TIMELESS FRIENDS

Forever and Always
The Timeless Bond of Friendship

By

Kathy Neaves

Dedication

To my cherished daughters, Amanda and Heather. Your steadfast support, joy, and affection have profoundly influenced my life in ways that words can never express. This book, "Timeless Friends," honors the connections we've nurtured and the memories we've built together. May it serve as a lasting reminder of the unique place you hold in my heart.

Amanda, your unwavering dedication as a mother of two daughters exemplifies love and protection in every aspect of your life. You have invested your heart into their upbringing, providing them with the essential tools they need to thrive. Your thoughtful parenting emphasizes core values like empathy, independence, respect, and accountability, fostering their growth and encouraging them to think critically. Through shared experiences and valued memories, you've instilled in them a sense of confidence to explore the world, making you an inspiring role model and a beacon of unconditional love.

Heather, you have an extraordinary perceptive, a brilliant individual whose warmth embraces all those around you. Your compassionate nature is evident in how you build relationships, always offering support and encouragement to those you hold dear. With your keen intellect, you approach challenges with creativity and insight, making you a natural problem solver in both personal and professional realms. Your kindness shines through in your actions; you listen with intent and empathize deeply, forging connections that uplift and motivate everyone around you. Your presence is a true blessing, reminding us all of the powerful impact of love and kindness in our lives.

This book, "Timeless Friends," embodies the joy and love you both bring into my life. May it forever remind you of our treasured moments and the unbreakable bond we share.

Always and Forever,

Mom

Acknowledgments

To my cherished friends who have been by my side through life's ups and downs,

This book lovingly acknowledges the unwavering sources of strength, the shining lights of hope, and the protectors of my heart. Your presence affirms the lasting power of genuine friendship.

In a world where connections can be transient, you have shown that some relationships are truly everlasting.

Your steadfast support, unconditional love, and relentless encouragement have formed the bedrock of my journey.

To those who have shared laughter, shed tears, and evolved alongside me, my gratitude knows no bounds. Your friendship serves as a reminder that even amidst chaos, there exists a sanctuary of home and belonging.

May this book stand as a homage to the beauty and resilience of your friendships. I hope it inspires others to value and cultivate the relationships that enrich our lives.

Thank you for being my eternal friends.

With heartfelt appreciation,

Kathy

Table of Contents

Chapter 1

Unexpected Connections

One sunny afternoon during the town's annual summer fair, Sarah and Luke met, sparking an unexpected and special friendship.

In the heart of the town, charming cottage-style houses exuded a unique charm and undeniable appeal. The well-worn brick sidewalks of Main Street transported visitors through time, evoking a nostalgic feeling and infusing the area with warmth and friendliness, embodying the genuine charm of a small town.

The peaceful sounds of birds chirping and leaves rustling created a strong sense of community among the residents.

Imagine the Umatilla River winding through the picturesque valley town. The soothing sounds of the crystal-clear waters cascading over smooth rocks brought a sense of peace. Sunlight danced on the river's surface, casting shimmering reflections of the majestic surroundings. The lush river bank was filled with vibrant colors, with willow trees arching their branches into the water and delicate white meadowfoam blossoms carpeting the fields, creating the illusion of frothy foam along the river's edge.

Every breath filled the air with the intoxicating fragrance of wildflowers, creating a symphony of scents that added to the charming allure of the idyllic setting.

Sarah wandered through the bustling fairgrounds, taking in the sights and sounds around her. The intricate details of handcrafted jewelry glistening in the sunlight and the tantalizing aroma of fresh baked goods wafting through the air captivated her.

Intrigued by the cheers and shouts, she turned her attention to a gathering of onlookers at the dunk tank, their laughter filling the air. A handsome young man wearing a playful smirk caught her eye as he encouraged his friends to dunk him, finding amusement in their missed attempts. A surge of camaraderie swelled within her, urging her to step forward and try her hand at dunking him.

The cold water and the sound of spectators' laughter sent a rush of excitement through her, quickening her heartbeat. A dilemma lingered in her mind—should she risk potential embarrassment or play it safe and let the opportunity pass?

Surveying the faces around her, her determination solidified. Ready to face the challenge, she took a deep breath and walked to the platform.

Her beauty was captivating, with long brown hair cascading in graceful waves around her face, accentuating her captivating blue eyes that radiated warmth and wisdom. Her infectious smile brightened the day of everyone she encountered, spreading joy like rays of sunlight.

As the boy saw her standing on the platform, his heart raced at her beauty. Her presence seemed to light up the entire fair ground, and her every move captivated him.

Sitting up straight, his eyes met hers as she approached. His tousled dark brown hair highlighted his solid and well-defined features, and his calm brown eyes exuded self-assurance.

Sarah's excitement reaches its peak as she clutches the ball, her eyes shining as she takes aim at the target; with a powerful throw, the ball leaves her hand and hits the target dead center.

In that moment, she realizes that the thrill of new experiences often comes from seizing opportunities and embracing the unknown.

Startled by the crowd, including the boy, the dunk tank releases a rush of water, sending him splashing into the tank with a loud splash. Sarah can't help but laugh at the sight of him soaked and sputtering water.

With water running down his face and clothes, he emerges from the dunk tank, breaking into a wide grin. With a slight blush, he joins in the laughter.

A surge of determination flows through him as he approaches her, eager to uncover the mystery behind her captivating eyes that had drawn him in.

Luke begins his introduction with a warm smile, his voice filled with anticipation. "Hey there, I'm Luke," his eyes gleaming as they meet hers.

She responds gracefully, extending her hand confidently, introducing herself: "I'm Sarah."

"Nice to meet you, Sarah," he says.

As the conversation unfolds, his curiosity leads him to ask, "Are your throwing skills part of a professional pursuit or just a leisurely hobby?"

Sarah's mischievous grin spreads across her face as she replies, "I'm just having fun showing off my dunking skills with style."

He can't help but add a playful wink to the lively conversation. He chuckles and shakes his head, feeling the water droplets flying from his ears.

"I'm impressed by the strength in your throw," he says, intrigued. "In the future, please handle me more delicately, like fragile glass that could break with the slightest touch?"

Sarah grins, her eyes twinkling with amusement. "It depends on whether you deserve it or not," she says. Luke finds her quick response thrilling and mysterious, stirring up excitement and anticipation. From that moment on, Sarah and Luke quickly become friends.

They spend the rest of the day exploring the unique attractions and enjoying a leisurely stroll through the bustling crowd.

As the sun sets, they find a spot by the town's picturesque lake and talk for hours about their dreams and aspirations. Their conversation flows as if their connection were timeless.

"Today was incredible, Sarah! I've loved getting to know you. I'd like to see you again."

"Luke, I had an amazing time too," she says, reaching for her phone with a gentle smile. "I was hoping you felt the same. Let me give you my contact information."

Luke grins gratefully and exclaims, "I can't wait to see where this journey takes us!"

"That's exactly what I was thinking!" Her tone brimming with enthusiasm. "But I should start heading home. My parents are expecting me soon."

With a confident smile, Luke locks eyes and says, "You can expect a call from me tomorrow."

Although Sarah and Luke were born and raised in the same hometown, their upbringing stories were vastly different from each other.

When Sarah returns home, she takes a moment to reflect on the events of the day. Overwhelmed with emotions, she feels excited about what the future holds for her and Luke.

Sarah's parents have dedicated their lives to helping those in need around the world. They are compassionate humanitarians who travel to impoverished nations to alleviate poverty.

Surrounded by a culture of giving, Sarah understood from a young age that living a purposeful life meant prioritizing actions over words.

Growing up, she embarked on numerous adventures with her parents, who not only raised her but also served as her mentors and closest companions, offering guidance and support throughout her journey. These experiences instilled in her a sense of curiosity and independence, fueling her passion for exploration and knowledge.

Upon returning home, Luke was overwhelmed by the events of the day. Reflecting on his encounters, he pondered whether Sarah could be the person he had been seeking. Her striking beauty and composed demeanor had left a lasting impression on him.

Filled with hope, he embraced the idea of creating something extraordinary with Sarah and eagerly anticipated uncovering their shared path.

Luke's father, a forward-thinking leader in the high-tech sector, was renowned for his visionary outlook and ability to anticipate future trends. His passion for innovation had positioned him as a trailblazer, with his strategic decision-making and bold initiatives not only transforming his company but also shaping the industry as a whole. His dedication to pioneering new ideas had earned him widespread respect and admiration in the high-tech realm.

Luke and his younger sister, Rachel, were raised in an environment that fostered creativity and resilience, with their parents encouraging them to embrace challenges and think outside the box.

In high school, Luke discovered his passion for entrepreneurship, laying the foundation for his future endeavors. He and Rachel engaged in friendly competition, pushing each other to achieve their goals and finding success in their respective ventures.

As summer drew to a close, Sarah and Luke's bond blossomed, bringing joy to their hearts and highlighting the profound impact of serendipitous connections.

With the start of a new school year, Sarah welcomed the opportunity for a fresh beginning, akin to an artist facing a blank canvas.

Eager to reunite with friends and embark on her senior year, Sarah looked forward to the possibilities that lay ahead, fueled by her love for learning, exploration, and personal growth.

Relieved from the summer heat, Sarah checked her schedule for the first day of school, spotting Luke by the entrance. With a smile on her face, she approached him, her footsteps echoing on the pavement.

"Good morning, Luke! It feels like just yesterday we were freshmen with endless possibilities."

Luke nodded in agreement, acknowledging the swift passage of time. "The new elective courses this year have caught my interest as well."

Excitement radiated from Sarah as she anticipated the year ahead.

"I've signed up for some fascinating classes, including a photography workshop," she shared enthusiastically. Turning to Luke, she asked, "What about you?"

After a brief pause, Luke replied, "I've enrolled in the coding class. It seems like it could lead to exciting opportunities in the future."

As they made their way to their first class, their conversation buzzed with anticipation for the opportunities that awaited them in the new school year.

Navigating the bustling hallways and encountering familiar faces, they experienced a mix of emotions as they embraced the responsibilities and freedoms that defined their senior year, with prom and graduation on the horizon, inspiring them to make the most of their final year.

Sarah's passion for science drove her to delve into the study of human anatomy, expanding her knowledge and expertise as she pursued her dream of becoming a cardiac surgeon. Supported by her teachers, who also served as mentors, she was commended for her unwavering dedication to her career aspirations.

Their biology teacher, Mr. Edwards, is a tall and commanding figure. He wears wire-framed glasses that rest on the bridge of his nose, and his salt-and-pepper hair exudes wisdom and expertise. The elbow patches on his tweed jacket give him an air of intellectual sophistication. Students admire and respect him for his dynamic teaching methods in biology, which include hands-on activities and demonstrations.

Mr. Edwards assigned Sarah and Luke to work together on a group project.

Sarah and Luke have been diligently working on their project, conducting research and engaging in deep conversations. Their collaboration has led to a lively exchange of ideas and expanded perspectives.

Both Sarah and Luke share a passion for biology and a fascination with the human body. Their teamwork thrives as they combine their interests and skills, motivating each other to explore new discoveries and pursue their aspirations. Luke admires Sarah's dedication and her goal of becoming a heart surgeon.

Feeling stressed about the approaching project deadline, Sarah found support from Luke. He acknowledged her concerns and suggested breaking the work into smaller tasks. Sarah agreed, and they met after school to complete the project.

Armed with textbooks and laptops, they gathered at a local coffee shop. Seated at a cozy corner table, surrounded by the rich aroma of brewed coffee and the sounds of chatter and clinking cups, they immersed themselves in their work.

Fueled by the barista's kindness in refilling their mugs, they channeled their motivation into creating an impressive project for their teacher.

Lost in their research, they discussed ideas and made written annotations, utilizing their time at the cafe to prepare their project.

After dedicating significant effort to collecting comprehensive data and conducting astute analyses, they felt a surge of pride as they put the finishing touches on their project.

Upon seeing their completed work, Mr. Edwards's eyes lit up with admiration. "Outstanding work, Sarah and Luke," he commended their thorough research and clear presentation. Their hard work and dedication did not go unnoticed, leaving them both with a sense of accomplishment and a renewed passion for science.

Sarah and Luke's unwavering support for each other brings joy to those around them, conquering the challenges of high school and providing steadfast encouragement during academic trials.

As they approach the final stretch of senior year, Sarah submits her university applications, each representing a potential future destination.

Sarah's high GPA reflects her dedication and academic excellence, instilling confidence as she awaits responses from prestigious institutions.

Embarking on her collegiate journey, she embraces the opportunities that lie ahead, demonstrating her commitment to excellence in each application.

As the deadline for acceptance letters nears, Sarah's anxiety mounts.

Checking her mailbox daily, Sarah eagerly anticipates a thick envelope that will pave the way for her higher education. Despite her nerves, she remains determined and focused, pouring her energy into her studies and activities as she awaits her future.

One afternoon, while sorting through her mail, Sarah spots a familiar logo on an envelope. Her hands tremble as she tears it open, her heart racing as she reads the words, "Congratulations! Johns Hopkins University is excited to welcome you to our pre-med program."

Gratitude and excitement wash over her as she shares the news with her parents and Luke. Luke's eyes shine with genuine happiness, his voice filled with whispers of pride. "I always knew you could do it."

Sarah's journey through the application process was transformative, showcasing her resilience, determination, and capacity for growth. As she prepares to embark on her college adventure, she does so with a renewed sense of purpose and optimism.

Her dream of attending pre-medical school has not only come true but has also surpassed her wildest expectations, as she has received a full scholarship to her top-choice program.

Sarah's world is full of possibilities, igniting excitement and wonder within her. Reflecting on the challenging journey that brought her to this point, she acknowledges her progress and embraces the path ahead with readiness to seize this opportunity.

Luke is grappling with uncertainty about his collegiate journey. Witnessing Sarah's joy at getting into Johns Hopkins prompts him to contemplate his potential role in his father's company and its impact on his future. He finds himself hesitant to commit to a specific path.

Standing in their caps and gowns as the sun sets, Sarah and Luke are poised for a new chapter. Excitement, nostalgia, and bitter sweetness fill the air as they reminisce about their high school years, marked by laughter, challenges, and unforgettable memories. Leaving behind familiar halls and faces, they eagerly anticipate an exciting, unknown future.

The valedictorian's speech inspired the graduating class to embrace their future paths and treasure their shared journey.

Listening to the speech, they realized they were embarking on a journey with boundless possibilities, armed with knowledge and friendships.

A moment of gratitude passed between Sarah and Luke as they walked across the stage to receive their well-deserved diplomas during the ceremony.

Pride radiates from Sarah's eyes, knowing she is on the brink of achieving her fervent ambition of becoming a renowned heart surgeon.

Sarah beams with pride as she exclaims to Luke, "We did it!"

Their remarkable journey culminates in triumphant success.

Luke beams with pride. "We have achieved it. Graduation is just the beginning of our future."

The bright horizon of what lies ahead unfolds like a vast highway with limitless opportunities and prospects.

An unbreakable bond of friendship unites Sarah and Luke, as they stand ready to face life's challenges with optimism and enthusiasm.

Chapter 2

Embracing The Unexpected Journey

As Sarah's departure date for university draws near, a mix of emotions and thoughts swirl within her, leading to introspection.

In just three weeks, she will embark on a new chapter. It feels like yesterday when she received that acceptance letter from Johns Hopkins. Is she prepared for this new journey? Will she be able to make new friends and handle the workload? Excitement and nervousness blend as she readies herself to enter a different world. She simply wants to be prepared for whatever lies ahead.

When Luke's truck pulled into the driveway with a rumble, its powerful engine caught her attention, prompting her to step outside to greet him.

With a warm smile, Sarah welcomed him and asked, "Would you like a refreshing drink?"

"Thank you! A refreshing drink is just what I need after a busy day," Luke replied.

"I'll be right back!" Sarah said as she headed off.

Luke settled into the rocking chair, taking in the peaceful surroundings. The sound of clinking glasses and the gentle pour of liquid filled the air as Sarah prepared their drinks.

Returning with a frosty glass of iced tea, Sarah offered it to Luke, the condensation glistening on the surface. "Here's your drink. I hope you enjoy it."

Luke's kind response was accompanied by a gentle smile and understanding eyes. "Thank you, Sarah." The soft creak of the rocking chairs and the distant chirping of birds created a calming atmosphere on the porch, perfect for relaxation.

"I'm glad to hear that! I love spending time outdoors, especially in the evenings," Sarah shared.

Expressing his gratitude, Luke said, "This tea is refreshing. You have a talent for making me feel welcome."

"It's my pleasure. How was your day? Anything interesting to share?" Sarah inquired.

Luke sighed. "Just the usual work routine, nothing too exciting. Being here with you is the highlight of my day."

Blushing, Sarah responded, "You're too kind. I always treasure our time together. Let's enjoy our tea and catch up some more."

Luke seizes the perfect moment to discuss his intention to enroll at Blue Mountain Community College. "Hey Sarah, I wanted to chat with you about my college plans."

Sarah turns to him. "I'm listening, Luke. What's on your mind?"

Luke takes a sip of his iced tea before speaking. "I've decided to start at a community college for two years and then transfer to pursue a business degree."

Sarah responds with enthusiasm. "That sounds like a solid plan! It's a smart way to save money on tuition and develop important skills."

"Yeah, it seems like the best choice for me. I appreciate your support."

"Of course, Luke. I believe in you, and I know that with determination, you will achieve your goals."

"Thank you, Sarah. Your encouragement means a lot to me. Beginning at a community college will set me up for success in the business field."

"I completely agree. You're making a wise decision, and I have no doubt that you will excel in the future. Stay focused and never lose sight of your dreams."

Sarah's validation of his decision gives Luke a sense of reassurance.

Luke feels grateful to have Sarah by his side. "Your confidence in me is motivating, Sarah. I won't let you down."

Sarah and Luke sit in comfortable silence, enjoying each other's company. The soothing sound of crickets fills the air, creating a peaceful atmosphere. As the sky darkens, Sarah leans back in her chair and gazes at the emerging stars. Luke reaches for Sarah's hand, intertwining their fingers, symbolizing their unspoken bond. Time seems to stand still, capturing their connection under the night sky.

With a playful look in his eyes, Luke turns to Sarah with a suggestion. "I have an idea." He smirks.

Intrigued, Sarah raises an eyebrow, knowing that Luke's ideas often lead to exciting adventures. "What are you thinking?"

Luke leans in. "Let's go on a road trip. Just the two of us, no plans or destination. Just the open road and whatever adventures come our way."

Excitement lights up Sarah's eyes at the prospect of embarking on a spontaneous journey with her best friend. Without hesitation, she nods, her heart racing at the unknown adventures that await.

The next morning, they pack a few essentials into Luke's vintage pickup truck and set off on their adventure. Filled with laughter, music, and shared stories, they feel a special connection as they cruise through miles of open road.

As the sun began to set, they found themselves in a charming town nestled in the mountains. Intrigued by its beauty, they decided to stay the night and explore its hidden gems.

Walking down the cobblestone streets, the sound of their footsteps echoed in the peaceful atmosphere. The old buildings towered over them, creating a sense of awe as shadows danced along the pathways. Each intricate detail of the historic architecture invited them to admire the beauty of a bygone era. Lost in the town's enchanting charm, they wandered, immersing themselves in the rich history that surrounded them. Strolling the cobblestone streets felt like a captivating journey back in time.

A quaint coffee shop caught Sarah's eye, and they settled at a table under a shady umbrella, enjoying the cozy ambiance and the aroma of freshly brewed coffee. The charming character of the coffee shop enhanced their experience.

Luke suggested, "What do you think about extending our stay in this town, Sarah?"

Excitedly, Sarah replied, "Absolutely! I'm loving our time here. Let's explore more tomorrow."

Luke smiled, "That's a great idea. How about we start with a visit to the local museum?"

"Perfect! Then we can wander through the streets leisurely. I'm eager to try local cuisine and experience a cultural event. This town has so much to offer."

Sarah exclaimed, "I can't wait for all the exciting adventures ahead."

The next day, Sarah and Luke were eager to continue their adventure in the charming town. With anticipation and curiosity, they set off on their exploration, ready to discover new sights and experiences.

As the sun rose higher, their excitement grew, fueling their desire to immerse themselves in the town's history and culture. Each corner revealed a new surprise, a new delight waiting to be uncovered. The town seemed to come alive with every step they took, offering them a glimpse into its past and present. With open hearts and wide eyes, they cherished every moment, creating lasting memories in this enchanting place.

After a satisfying lunch, they stumbled upon the town's modest museum. James, a proud local resident and descendant of early settlers, shared fascinating stories about his family's life in the late 1890s. The scent of old wood and ancient artifacts filled the air as visitors marveled at the relics from the once-thriving coal mines. The display of tools and machinery told the stories of hardworking miners from a bygone era.

This encounter deepened their respect for the laborers who worked in the mines in the past.

Ending their day with a leisurely walk along the cobblestone streets, they discovered a cozy, family-owned restaurant. While enjoying their meal, they realized it was time to head home the next day. Sarah looked at Luke with gratitude, feeling a sense of connection and appreciation. In that moment, she felt thankful for his presence in her life. The warmth in his eyes and the curve of his smile conveyed a deep bond that went beyond words. She felt his friendship in the gentle squeeze of his hand, a silent reassurance of their connection.

Luke, I want to express my gratitude for suggesting this road trip. It's been exactly what I needed," Sarah said, finishing her meal. "I'm so happy to hear that, Sarah. You're going to achieve great things at John Hopkins, and I'm thankful we could have this adventure before you begin this new chapter," Luke replied with a warm smile. Their hands occasionally touched, conveying a sense of warmth and comfort, symbolizing the strong bond they had developed through their shared experiences.

The sunrise painted streaks of color across the horizon as Sarah and Luke journeyed back home. They shared joy and laughter, stopping at charming spots to admire the picturesque countryside. The beauty of their surroundings reflected the beauty of their friendship, making each moment together even more special. With each mile traveled, they treasured the memories and the connection they shared, creating lasting moments to carry with them beyond the road trip.

As they approached home, Sarah turned to Luke with curiosity. "When do your classes start at the community college?"

"I'm excited to start my classes at the community college next week."

"You're eager to begin this new chapter in your life."

Luke's smile widened, his eyes filled with anticipation. "Absolutely! When do you leave for Johns Hopkins?"

Sarah furrowed her brows in thought, scanning the road ahead. "I plan to head east in about a week."

"I'll miss you, Sarah. Let's keep in touch while we're at school."

Sarah nodded. "That sounds like a plan. It's important to stay connected even when we're apart."

Upon arriving at Sarah's house, she turned to Luke. "I'm proud of you for pursuing your education. I know you'll thrive at the community college."

"Thank you, Sarah. I have no doubt you'll excel at Johns Hopkins. You'll make a fantastic doctor one day."

They embraced tightly, knowing that their friendship would endure despite the distance. As they bid farewell, they realized that this marked the beginning of exciting adventures ahead.

Chapter 3

New Beginnings at John Hopkins Embracing the Promise of Academic

Sarah's journey at Johns Hopkins begins with a memorable occasion filled with obstacles, victories, and a profound sense of belonging to a scholarly community. From the moment she steps onto the campus, she is thrust into a whirlwind of new experiences, each adding a new layer to her personal and academic growth.

On her inaugural day at Johns Hopkins University, Sarah experiences a whirlwind of emotions. She feels a blend of anticipation and anxiety while maneuvering through the lively campus, the hustle and bustle around her serving as both a source of excitement and trepidation. She encounters students rushing to their lectures, groups animatedly discussing academic theories, and professors deeply engaged in scholarly debates. This vibrant environment heightens her senses, making every interaction, every glance at a new face, feel like an invitation to explore a world brimming with knowledge.

The invigorating autumn breeze seems to herald fresh starts as she heads to her initial lecture, the cool air awakening her senses, and the rustling leaves whispering promises of what is yet to come. Her thoughts are filled with the boundless opportunities awaiting her, a mix of academic challenges and the prospect of forming lifelong friendships. As she walks into her first lecture hall, the sight of rows of students and the soft hum of intellectual curiosity fills her with both a sense of belonging and a realization of the magnitude of the journey ahead.

Sarah embraces the dynamic university environment, enthralled by the lively atmosphere and the unquenchable desire for learning that permeates the esteemed institution. With every stride, she experiences a sense of entering a realm brimming with wisdom and development. Each classroom holds the potential for groundbreaking ideas, each lecture a stepping stone toward her future aspirations. She finds herself in awe of the professors, their expertise evident in every word they speak, and the students, whose dedication mirrors her own. It's a realm where possibilities are not just dreamed of but actively pursued.

However, amid this excitement, Sarah's heart aches with a profound longing, a yearning that even her constant communication with Luke can't fully ease. Their conversations become a lifeline, bridging the distance between them, and providing her with comfort in the midst of this new and challenging environment. The sincere warmth exuded by Luke's presence, even through the screen or a phone call, is unmatched. It's a feeling of home that she carries with her, a reminder of the support and love waiting for her beyond the campus boundaries.

Sarah feels her heart fill with joy as she reads Luke's messages. Their exchanges are more than just words; they are small moments of connection that bring her comfort amidst the chaos of university life. One evening, as she settles into her dorm room after a long day of lectures, her phone lights up with a message from Luke, proposing a weekend visit. The thought of their reunion immediately lifts her spirits.

Luke: Hi Sarah, If you are free this weekend, I'm planning to come and visit you. Are you available?

Sarah: Yes, Luke! I have no plans for the weekend.

Luke: I miss hanging out with you. Any special plans while I'm around?

Sarah: How about we go for a hike and then have dinner downtown?

Luke: That sounds fantastic! I'm eager to catch up and spend time with you.

Sarah: Me too. I look forward to seeing you this weekend.

The thought of their reunion brings her comfort and joy. She can't help but smile as she envisions the fun they will have together. Memories of their past adventures flash through her mind, and she finds herself daydreaming about the peacefulness of their upcoming hike and the laughter-filled conversations they will share over dinner. The idea of treasuring special moments with him fills her heart with a sense of contentment, adding a silver lining to her busy academic schedule.

After delving into a week of immunology and microbiology lectures, Sarah feels mentally and emotionally drained. The complexity of the subjects leaves her yearning for a respite, a break from the rigor of academic life. Luke's arrival seems like the perfect remedy, a chance for her to unwind and recharge. She eagerly anticipates the weekend, imagining the moments of peace and relaxation they will share, offering her a much-needed breather from the demands of her studies.

Luke's messages continue to provide her with comfort and inspiration throughout the week. His words are like a soothing balm to her anxiety, empowering her and confirming that she is not alone in her journey. In moments of doubt, his messages serve as a reminder of his unwavering support. They act as a beacon of hope, affirming her readiness to face the upcoming trials and challenges of university life.

As the weekend approaches, Sarah's anticipation grows. She eagerly awaits Luke's arrival, knowing that their time together will be filled with new adventures and cherished memories. The thought of fresh experiences with him thrills her, offering a rejuvenating respite from the week's obligations. Every minute leading up to his arrival feels like an eternity, but it also builds up the excitement, making their impending reunion all the more special.

When Sarah's phone illuminates with an incoming call from Luke, her heart skips a beat with happiness. She answers with an eagerness that is almost palpable. "Hello, Luke!" she exclaims, her voice brimming with excitement.

"Hey, Sarah," Luke replies warmly. "Just wanted to give you a heads-up that my flight is boarding, and I'll be arriving at 4:20. I can't wait to see you soon!"

A wave of combined relief and excitement washes over Sarah. "I'll be seeing you," she replies, her voice laced with anticipation.

As he boards the plane, Luke's mind races with thoughts of their reunion. Anticipation builds within him as he imagines their time together, the joy of being able to reconnect after weeks apart. Sarah, on the other hand, counts down the minutes until his arrival, her heart swelling with happiness at the thought of seeing him again.

With each glance at the clock, Sarah imagines the moments they will share, feeling a surge of warmth and excitement. The thought of Luke's imminent arrival brings her overwhelming joy, filling her with a sense of happiness that she hasn't felt in weeks. She hurries to the terminal to meet him, her steps quickening with each passing moment. When his plane finally touches down, her excitement becomes contagious, spreading to those around her as she eagerly awaits their reunion.

As Luke descends the escalator, Sarah watches with bated breath. His enthusiastic presence fills the terminal with warmth, and as their eyes meet, her smile lights up the room, evoking laughter and joyful melodies that echo the depth of their special bond. Their reunion is charged with intense emotions, their wordless glances capturing their deep connection and the intimate moment they are sharing.

"Luke, this moment is precious to me! Your smile brings me such happiness," Sarah expresses, her eyes gleaming with joy. Luke's eyes soften as he replies, "I've missed you, Sarah." Their voices are low, almost lost amidst the noise of the terminal, yet in that moment, the world around them seems to fade away.

Excitement builds as they walk toward Sarah's car in the parking lot, catching up on each other's lives. The air between them is filled with laughter and heartfelt exchanges. Amid the reunion, Sarah suddenly realizes her hunger, her stomach rumbling audibly.

"Luke, I'm craving pizza right now," she admits with a laugh.

"What pizza do you want?" Luke asks, his eyes lighting up at the idea.

"At first, I was thinking of going with a classic pepperoni, but I'm open to trying different toppings. How about you?" Sarah says.

"I enjoy Hawaiian pizza, so how about we order one of each and divide it?" Luke suggests with a grin.

"That sounds delicious. I love trying different pizzas," Sarah responds, her eyes gleaming with excitement.

The bustling pizzeria pulses with the vibrant energy of a Friday night. The enticing scent of freshly baked pizza fills the air, harmonizing with the sounds of orders being taken and dishes clattering. Seated outside under a cheerful umbrella, they find a moment of tranquility amidst the lively cityscape. The fusion of city allure and the delicious aroma of pizza creates an atmosphere of warmth and relaxation, enveloping them in an experience to savor.

As they share their meal, Luke inquires about her week. "Sarah, how did your classes and lectures go this week?" His voice is filled with genuine interest.

Sarah describes her week with animated gestures, detailing thought-provoking discussions in her anatomy class and fascinating insights from a guest lecture on immunology and microbiology. Luke listens attentively, nodding and offering words of encouragement. Their conversation flows effortlessly, marked by mutual respect and a sincere curiosity about each other's experiences. It's in these moments that Sarah realizes how much she has missed having Luke by her side, his presence providing a sense of comfort and normalcy.

After leaving the pizzeria, they embark on a relaxing drive through the city, admiring the bright skyline and the bustling streets. The evening air is crisp, the city lights casting a soft glow that reflects the excitement they both feel. When they reach the hotel, they finalize their plans for the hike the next day, feeling their anticipation grow with every passing second. Luke embraces her before parting ways for the night, his touch lingering as they prepare for their adventure ahead.

At the break of dawn, the soft sunlight peeks through the window, painting Luke's room in a warm, cozy glow. A rush of enthusiasm fills him as he grabs his phone to message Sarah, picturing the day unfolding before them. He sends a brief message to confirm their hiking plans, assuring her of his punctuality. Sarah soon arrives at the hotel, her excitement evident as she calls him. "Are you ready to leave?" she asks eagerly.

"I'm on my way out!" Luke replies, his voice filled with anticipation.

Sarah and Luke set out on a scenic excursion to Lake Roland Natural Council, an oasis of tranquility located a mere four miles away from the lively university campus. The towering trees and shimmering waters create a serene haven, offering a soothing escape from their scholarly pursuits and the pressures of campus life. Eager to explore the unspoiled beauty of the lake, they anticipate making lasting memories in its peaceful surroundings.

As they walk along the picturesque trails, they find themselves reflecting on the journey so far. Sarah's inaugural year at Johns Hopkins is drawing to a close, a thought that fills her with a mix of excitement and nostalgia. With summer break approaching, thoughts of returning home swirl in her mind. The tranquil surroundings mirror her sense of anticipation and wonder, providing the perfect backdrop for their conversation.

With a hint of excitement in her voice, Sarah shares her plans with Luke. "I've been thinking about volunteering at St. Anthony's hospital this summer," she says.

Luke beams with support. "That's fantastic, Sarah! What inspired you to make this decision?"

"Given my passion for the medical field, I see it as a valuable chance to get hands-on experience. Duke University School of Medicine values candidates with experience in medical settings," Sarah explains, her eyes shining with determination.

"That's a smart move, Sarah. It shows your dedication to your future aspirations," Luke nods in agreement.

"I'm optimistic that by volunteering at St. Anthony's, I can gain valuable insights and contribute to the patients' lives there," Sarah adds, her voice filled with hope.

"You'll excel at this opportunity, Sarah. It's a fantastic way to prepare for your future in the medical field," Luke reassures her, his words filled with conviction.

After hours of exploring the trails, Sarah and Luke emerge from nature's embrace, ready to refuel. They discuss their plans for the rest of the day as they search for a charming spot for lunch. The sun casts a warm glow, setting the stage for a leisurely meal and discussions about their evening plans.

With Sunday morning on the horizon, Luke's thoughts drift towards his journey back home. Surrounded by nature's tranquility, they find solace in each other's company, looking forward to future adventures. During lunch at a neighborhood deli, Sarah looks at Luke with curiosity. "Luke, would you like to go to a cookout at one of my classmates' this evening?"

"That sounds like a lot of fun, Sarah. I'm eager to meet your university companions!" Luke replies with enthusiasm.

Later that afternoon, they arrive at the cookout. The aroma of grilled food fills the air, and they quickly spot Sarah's friend, Cassie. "Oh my gosh, Cassie! I didn't know you were coming to the cookout, too," Sarah exclaims.

As they engage in friendly banter, Cassie turns her attention to Luke. "Who's this handsome guy with you?" she asks with a teasing smile.

Sarah introduces Luke, and the two exchange warm greetings. The evening unfolds in a blur of laughter and conversations, the three of them finding common ground and creating new memories.

Over the weekend, Sarah and Luke savor every moment together. The time they spend together becomes a cherished memory, a blend of shared experiences and the unspoken bond that ties them together. However, the weekend also brings with it the inevitable farewell.

The next day, as they drive to the airport, a heavy silence fills the car. Luke gazes out the window, his mind already miles away. The weight of their impending separation hangs in the air. As they stop, they turn to each other, their eyes filled with unspoken words of love and longing. They embrace, clinging to one another as if wishing time would pause.

"Sarah, I want to thank you for everything. You've been such an important part of my life, and I'm grateful for all the memories we've shared," Luke says, his voice tinged with emotion.

"Luke, you're going to make me emotional. I'll be home soon, and we will have the entire summer to spend together," Sarah replies, fighting back her tears.

As they part, Sarah watches Luke fade into the crowd, a pang of sorrow gripping her heart. Their farewell marks the beginning of a new chapter in their poignant love story.

Luke returns to college, eager for Sarah's return. He secures a summer job at his family's high-tech business, applying his academic skills and preparing for the challenges ahead. Meanwhile, Sarah's excitement is all but containable as she begins her volunteer work at St. Anthony's. The summer ahead promises to be fulfilling and rewarding as she dedicates herself to helping others and embracing the carefree spirit of the season.

Sarah enjoys her time at St. Anthony's, engaging in patient care and helping in the cardiology wing. She finds joy in the simple pleasures of the season—savoring fresh fruits, watching sunsets, and creating cherished memories. As she navigates this chapter, she embraces the warmth and tranquility of summer, ready to face whatever comes next.

Chapter 4

Paths to Purpose and Continuing Commitments - Luke's Internship and Sarah's Medical School Journey

Sarah focuses on her studies and volunteering at St. Anthony's throughout her summer breaks for the next three years, driven by her dream of attending Duke

University's cardiology program. Each summer, she dives into her responsibilities with unwavering determination, embracing every opportunity to learn and grow. She often finds herself engrossed in complex medical cases, asking questions, and taking meticulous notes that she later reviews during her study sessions. Her commitment is evident in how she meticulously balances her time between volunteering, studying for exams, and maintaining a connection with her mentors and peers.

Her schedule is packed with challenging courses, late-night studying, and practical clinical training, all meticulously planned to prepare her for the demanding application process to Duke. She dives into advanced coursework in anatomy, physiology, and biochemistry, often burning the midnight oil in the library, poring over medical journals and textbooks. Her evenings are spent in the hospital, where she learns the intricacies of patient care, observes surgeries, and assists doctors in the cardiology wing. Sarah's commitment to her dream is unshakable; even the most exhausting days don't deter her. She finds solace in the incremental progress she makes, each skill learned and each piece of knowledge gained reinforcing her confidence.

Anticipation fills her as she envisions her journey to becoming a skilled surgeon at Duke University. She often imagines herself standing in an operating room, the hum of machines around her and a team of skilled surgeons at her side. These daydreams fuel her, driving her to push through the moments of doubt and fatigue. She writes her goals in a journal, each entry a promise to herself to persevere, regardless of the challenges that lie ahead.

In the meantime, Luke completes his studies at Blue Mountain Community College, earning his Associate's Degree with a sense of accomplishment and pride. His passion for business drives him to make the bold decision to transfer to the University of Oregon (UO) to pursue his Bachelor's in Business Administration. This decision is not made lightly; Luke has long been fascinated by the complexities of running a business, particularly his family's. He spends hours researching UO's business program, carefully planning his next steps to ensure they align with his career aspirations.

With a firm foundation and a clear vision for his future, Luke is ready to excel at UO and, ultimately, in the business world. He approaches his studies with a strategic mindset, focusing on courses that will provide him with the skills and knowledge necessary to lead his family business into the future. His determination and ambition are palpable, and he quickly becomes known among his peers and professors as someone who is not only talented but also deeply committed to his goals. Luke's confidence grows with each passing semester, propelling him towards a successful and fulfilling career.

Luke's internship at St. Anthony's HR department during his final year at UO becomes a pivotal moment in his professional growth. He initially feels a mix of excitement and apprehension, recognizing this experience as a crucial step toward achieving his career goals. While he has aspirations of leading his family business, he sees the internship as a valuable opportunity to gain insights into organizational management, human resources, and the intricacies of healthcare administration from a unique vantage point.

This duality of ambition underscores his commitment to both personal and professional development. The internship challenges him to step outside his comfort zone, requiring him to balance his passion for business with the realities of managing people and navigating the complexities of healthcare. It's not always easy, but Luke approaches each task with enthusiasm and a strong work ethic, eager to absorb as much knowledge as possible. He quickly becomes a valuable asset to the team at St. Anthony's, contributing innovative ideas and demonstrating a knack for problem-solving that impresses his supervisors.

With a passion for making a meaningful impact in his community, Luke is determined to make the most of this learning opportunity. He works closely with the HR team, helping to implement new policies and streamline processes. He takes on projects that allow him to apply his academic knowledge in a practical setting, such as developing staff training programs and assisting in the recruitment process. His commitment to excellence and his drive to contribute to the hospital's mission make him stand out, and he starts to see how his efforts can create positive change within the organization.

Meanwhile, Sarah's acceptance into Duke Medical University marks an exhilarating new chapter in her journey toward becoming a cardiothoracic surgeon. Receiving her acceptance letter is a moment of triumph, one that brings tears to her eyes as she reads the words she has longed to see. The distance between home and Duke, however, adds a layer of complexity to this milestone. While the achievement fills her with pride, it also brings a deep sense of longing and discomfort, knowing that her journey will take her further from Luke and her familiar surroundings.

Despite the demands of her studies, Sarah's commitment to volunteering at St. Anthony's during her summer breaks showcases her unwavering dedication to making a difference in the lives of others. Her work at the hospital is more than just a resume builder; it is a testament to her passion for medicine and her desire to give back to the community that has supported her journey. She takes on more responsibilities each summer, mentoring new volunteers and taking on complex tasks in the cardiology wing. As she immerses herself in this new phase of her education, Sarah's passion for helping others remains a guiding force, promising a bright and impactful future in medicine.

Her actions reflect her caring nature and ambition to create positive change. Each patient she assists, each procedure she observes, further solidifies her decision to pursue a career in cardiology. Sarah dedicates herself to her studies at Duke, aiming to not only excel academically but also to use her skills to serve the community and improve the lives of her patients. Her days are filled with rigorous academic challenges, but she finds fulfillment in knowing that each lesson learned brings her one step closer to making a real impact in the world.

One warm, serene summer evening, Sarah heads to St. Anthony's with a sense of contentment. As the sun dips below the horizon, casting a golden glow over the tranquil landscape, she takes a moment to appreciate the world around her. The gentle hum of cicadas fills the air, and a soft breeze carries the scent of freshly cut grass. On her way to work, Sarah savors the beauty of the summer evening, grateful for these moments of peace amid her hectic life. The fading light paints the sky in hues of pink and orange, creating a breathtaking backdrop for her journey. Despite the impending shift, she finds solace in the evening's peacefulness, allowing herself to be enveloped in the warmth and tranquility of the season.

As Sarah smooths out the wrinkles in her volunteer uniform, her heart buzzes with a familiar blend of excitement and determination. Each visit to St. Anthony's brings her closer to her goal of becoming a cardiothoracic surgeon. She pauses for a moment near the entrance, taking in the bustling scene that has become both familiar and comforting. Families huddle in waiting rooms, nurses glide between patients, and the occasional beeping of medical equipment fills the air with a sense of urgency and hope.

"Sarah, could you grab these charts for Dr. Thompson?" calls out a nurse from the front desk, snapping Sarah back to reality.

"Of course," Sarah replies with a bright smile, striding toward the nurse. "Thank you, Cindy."

As she walks toward the cardiology wing, her thoughts drift to her best friend, Luke. They have shared so much over the years, from intense study sessions to whimsical road trips. His unwavering support has been one of her greatest strengths, helping her through moments of doubt and exhaustion. Luke, chasing his dreams of leading his family business, always finds time to lift her spirits with his infectious optimism and witty remarks.

Reaching the designated room, Sarah hesitates for a split second before knocking. She steps inside to find a young woman about her age, engrossed in a medical textbook, her expression one of deep concentration. The girl looks up, and a spark of recognition passes between them.

"Hi, I'm Sarah. Are you new here?" Her voice exudes a comforting and welcoming warmth.

The girl smiles, setting aside her book. "Yes, I am Jessica. It's nice to meet you, Sarah."

"Likewise. What brings you here?" Sarah asks, curious about this unfamiliar face.

Jessica's eyes light up with a passion that mirrors Sarah's own. "I'm here for volunteer work, too. My dream is to become a cardiothoracic surgeon one day."

Sarah feels an immediate connection. "No way! That's my dream as well. St. Anthony's is an excellent learning place."

The conversation flows between them as they exchange stories and motivations. Sarah finds herself invigorated by Jessica's shared passion. For the first time, she feels not only inspired by her own goals but also challenged by Jessica's determination. Their interactions breathe new life into her aspirations, and she realizes how enriching it is to have a peer who shares her dreams.

The rest of the shift flies by as Jessica and Sarah work together, developing a friendly competition. They challenge each other to perform their tasks with precision and efficiency, but always with a spirit of camaraderie. By the end of the night, they have formed a bond, one built on mutual respect and a shared vision for their futures. As their shift ends, they walk out of the hospital side by side. Jessica glances at Sarah and says, "This is the start of something special."

"You're right, Jessica. It's not every day you meet someone with the same dream," Sarah agrees.

They exchange phone numbers, promising to keep in touch and support each other's journey. As Sarah walks toward her car, she can't help but feel that her path has become a little brighter and a lot more exciting. The addition of Jessica into her life adds a new layer to her journey, one that fills her with renewed enthusiasm.

When Sarah arrives home, her phone buzzes with a message from Luke. "How was your shift?" it reads.

She types a reply: "Amazing! I met someone named Jessica who also aspires to be a cardiothoracic surgeon. Feels like I've found a partner in crime. Can't wait to tell you all about it."

Luke's response is immediate: "Sounds outstanding! Let's catch up soon."

Sarah smiles and sets her phone down, feeling an overwhelming sense of gratitude for the people in her life who share her journey. Her parents have worked hard to provide her with an excellent education and support her dream of becoming a cardiothoracic surgeon. She reflects on the sacrifices they've made and their unwavering belief in her abilities, knowing that she wouldn't be where she is today without their support.

Sarah grew up in an environment where her parents encouraged her to strive for excellence. Their active involvement in both the local community and on a global scale served as an inspiration for her to aspire to make a positive impact on the world. Their support motivated her to aim high and believe in herself, instilling in her a sense of responsibility to use her talents for the greater good. Her parents' passion for making a difference became a guiding force in her life, influencing her desire to contribute to society through her work in medicine.

A cloudless cerulean sky accompanies the weekend. The sun shines brightly, enveloping everything it touches in a welcoming, warm glow. The air is dry and balmy, carrying the pleasant fragrance of freshly mown grass and blooming flowers. Verdant trees stand in full bloom, their leaves rustling in the soft breeze. Cheerful birds flit from branch to branch, filling the air with their joyful chirping.

Sarah has been eagerly anticipating this day, a break from the hospital to relax and catch up with Luke. The plan is straightforward: a coffee date at their go-to cafe followed by a leisurely walk through the park. Luke had been adamant that he had something important to discuss, stirring Sarah's curiosity. As she approaches the cafe, she spots Luke already seated at their usual table by the window. With a familiar grin spreading across his face, he waves at Sarah. Her heart lifts at his infectious energy.

She slides into the seat opposite him, setting her bag down with a light thud. "Hey, Luke! I'm glad we could meet." Their busy schedules make each meetup feel like a minor victory, a stolen moment of normalcy amid the chaos of their lives.

"Hey, Sarah! You look radiant as always," Luke says, his eyes sparkling with mischief. "I've got something exciting to tell you."

"Oh, do you?" Sarah raises an eyebrow, leaning in with genuine curiosity. "Tell!"

Luke takes a sip of his coffee before diving into the subject. "Do you remember me telling you about Professor Anderson? The business whiz who gave that incredible lecture at UO last year?"

Sarah nods in agreement, recalling the conversation about Luke's professor, whose advice on life and career had resonated with many of Luke's classmates. "Yes, I remember. What about him?" she says.

"Well, guess what? He's agreed to be my mentor for the year!" Luke's face lights up with excitement. "And get this—he knows a renowned cardiothoracic surgeon. I thought he could introduce you two."

Sarah's eyes widen in amazement. "Are you serious? That could change things for me. What's the catch?"

Luke laughs. "No catch. Professor Anderson is all about helping ambitious students like us. He sees potential and wants to nurture it. I figured, why not extend that opportunity to you?"

For a moment, Sarah sits in awe, absorbing the enormity of Luke's offer. She feels her heart swell with gratitude and a renewed sense of purpose. "Luke, this is incredible. Thank you. I'm speechless."

"Just say you'll meet him," Luke replies with a chuckle. "I've already set up a meeting for the three of us tomorrow. Are you free?"

Sarah's voice trembles with excitement. "Yes! Oh my gosh, this could be the break I've been waiting for."

They spend the rest of their time at the cafe discussing the upcoming meeting, speculating on what the mentor might say, and dreaming about their futures. With Luke by her side, Sarah feels invincible. His unwavering support and enthusiasm give her the confidence to overcome any challenge that comes her way.

The next day arrives with a flurry of nervous anticipation. Sarah dresses with meticulous care, choosing an outfit that strikes the right balance between professionalism and approachability. She can't shake the feeling that this is something monumental, a defining moment in her journey.

Luke picks her up, and they drive to Professor Anderson's office at the university. Upon arriving, the professor ushers them into a cozy, cluttered room filled with books and inspirational signs, greeting them with a warm smile.

"Good to see you, Luke," Professor Anderson says, extending his hand. "And you must be Sarah. Luke has told me a lot about you."

"I'm honored to meet you, Professor Anderson," Sarah says, shaking his hand.

"Likewise," he says, gesturing for them to sit. "Now, let's get down to business. I've arranged for you to meet Dr. Aaron Blake. He's one of the top cardiothoracic surgeons at St. Anthony's and a close friend. He's agreed to mentor you in whatever capacity he can."

Professor Anderson hands Sarah a piece of paper with Dr. Blake's contact information. "He's expecting your call," he says with a reassuring smile.

Sarah feels a surge of gratitude. "Thank you so much, Professor Anderson. This means the world to me."

After discussing their plans for mentorship and future goals, Sarah and Luke leave the office buzzing with excitement. As they walk out, the sun is setting, casting a golden glow over the campus.

"Can you believe this is happening?" Sarah says, her voice barely above a whisper.

"Believe it," Luke says. "We're on our way to achieving our dreams, one step at a time."

As they return to Luke's car, Sarah pulls out her phone and dials Dr. Blake's number, her heart pounding as she waits for the call to connect.

"Hello, this is Dr. Blake," a deep, calm voice says.

"Hi, Dr. Blake, my name is Sarah. Professor Anderson mentioned you might provide some mentorship. I'm passionate about becoming a cardiothoracic surgeon, and I would love any guidance you could offer."

A brief pause follows, and Dr. Blake says, "Yes, Sarah. Anderson spoke highly of you. I'd be happy to help. Let's arrange a meeting at St. Anthony's. How does tomorrow afternoon sound?"

Sarah's heart races with excitement. "That sounds perfect, Dr. Blake. Thank you so much. I'll see you then."

Sarah hangs up, turning to Luke with a jubilant smile. "It's happening. I'm meeting him tomorrow."

"I'm so proud of you, Sarah," Luke says, pulling her into a tight hug. "You've got this."

As Sarah drives home, she feels like she is floating on air. Her dreams are within reach, and she knows that with the support of her friends and family, she can conquer anything that comes her way.

The following day, Sarah meets with Dr. Blake at St. Anthony's. Excitement and nerves bubble up as she stands in front of his office door. Taking a deep breath to calm herself, she knocks on the door.

"Come in," Dr. Blake says.

"Good afternoon, Dr. Blake. I'm Sarah," she says, extending her hand.

"Nice to meet you, Sarah. I'm eager to hear about your plans and how I can help," Dr. Blake says, gesturing for her to take a seat.

"I've been volunteering here at St. Anthony's during my summer breaks throughout my time at Johns Hopkins University," Sarah begins. "It's helped me gain so much insight into the medical field. I look forward to coming back to complete my fellowship in a couple of years. The opportunity to contribute to the community that has been a pillar of support throughout my journey fills me with a deep sense of pride."

Dr. Blake listens attentively as Sarah speaks, her words flowing with passion and sincerity. He can see the drive and determination in her eyes, recognizing the qualities that make a great surgeon.

"Sarah, my next appointment is in 15 minutes," Dr. Blake says with sincerity in his voice. "Despite the time constraints, I would love to continue our conversation at a later time." He writes his personal phone number on a piece of paper and hands it to her with a warm smile, assuring her of his availability to assist whenever needed. "Let's get together later this week. I'm interested in learning more about your journey."

This small but meaningful gesture leaves Sarah feeling appreciated and encouraged, confident that she has found a compassionate and committed ally in Dr. Blake.

"Thank you, Dr. Blake. I'll call later this week to see when you are available."

As Sarah expresses her gratitude, her sincerity radiates through her words, leaving a lasting impression on him. Her heartfelt gestures underscore the significance of their interaction, leaving him with a deep sense of appreciation for her in return.

Upon exiting Dr. Blake's office, a wave of confidence and reassurance envelops Sarah. The burdensome weight she had been carrying dissipates, replaced by a sense of excitement and purpose.

Sarah looks forward to recounting every detail of her uplifting news. Bubbled with excitement, she dials Luke's number, eager to share the positive news.

"Luke, I had an exceptional appointment with Dr. Blake today! I am absolutely delighted!" Sarah's enthusiasm is palpable as she shares the news with Luke.

"I'm genuinely happy for you, Sarah. How about we meet for lunch tomorrow to celebrate and reconnect? I'll send you a message when I'm ready for my break."

Sarah hangs up the phone and begins preparing for the next day. After dinner, she arranges her volunteer uniform and packs her bag with essentials for the hospital. With a sense of purpose and dedication, she readies herself, ensuring she will be prepared to offer help and comfort to patients in need.

As she heads to bed early, her mind fills with anticipation for the day ahead. She knows that being well-rested will allow her to be at her best, ready to provide support and care to those who rely on the hospital's services. With a mixture of excitement and determination, Sarah drifts off to sleep, eager to make a difference in the lives of the patients she will meet the next day.

As the alarm clock blares at 6:00 am, Sarah springs out of bed and dresses for the day ahead. With a sense of purpose, she prepares a steaming cup of coffee and spreads cream cheese on a toasted bagel for a satisfying breakfast. She assembles her lunch for work, ensuring she has everything she needs for the day. With a bright smile and a positive outlook, Sarah embraces the new day that awaits her.

When Sarah arrives at the hospital, her warm and compassionate nature is evident as she greets everyone with genuine care and concern. "Morning, Cindy, how was your weekend?" she asks, her friendly smile putting others at ease.

"Morning, Sarah," Cindy replies with a nod, a warm smile lighting up her face. "My weekend was wonderful."

Sarah's thoughtfulness shines through as she looks forward to seeing Luke at the hospital later in the day. Her kind and nurturing demeanor brings comfort to those around her, reinforcing the impact she has on both patients and colleagues.

Sarah lifts the patient files from the nurses' station, a tangible reminder of the immense responsibility she shoulders. Moving with purpose through the hospital halls toward the cardiac unit, where every second counts, she senses the gravity of the situation. A brief encounter with Dr. Blake, a respected cardiologist, is more than just cordial greetings; it signifies a shared dedication to the noble mission of restoring health and preserving lives.

Sarah approaches Ms. Walters' door with a gentle knock, understanding the fragility of the woman recovering from open-heart surgery. "How are you feeling, Ms. Walters?" she asks, her voice soft and filled with genuine concern.

Ms. Walters' eyes reflect a hint of relief as she responds, "I'm feeling much better today. Thank you." This simple exchange captures the essence of empathy and compassion, illustrating the power of human connection in moments of vulnerability.

"Is there anything you need this morning?" Sarah inquires.

Sitting up in her bed, Ms. Walters responds with a soft smile, "Yes, if you don't mind, I would love for you to open my blinds. I would like to see the sunshine."

As Sarah obliges, she notices Ms. Walters' water cup is empty. Without hesitation, she refills the cup, ensuring her comfort and well-being.

"You are showing wonderful progress," Sarah says as she departs from Ms. Walters' room. "I am confident that you will go home tomorrow. Dr. Blake will visit you soon. Take care and rest well."

As Sarah walks down the hospital wing, her phone chimes with a message from Luke, inviting her to join him for lunch in the cafeteria. Overjoyed at the chance to meet him and share a few moments, Sarah quickly agrees.

Chapter 5

New Horizons - Embracing Opportunities and Challenges

Sarah and Luke are well-prepared to start new stages in their lives, eager to embrace the opportunities and challenges that lie ahead as they pursue their individual goals. St. Anthony's promoted Luke to Assistant Director of Human Resources, and he dedicates himself to fostering a harmonious work environment. Every day at St. Anthony's gives him the opportunity to grow and improve in both personal and professional aspects of his life. He forges meaningful connections with his team, demonstrating the importance of valuing their input and working together to find solutions that enhance their professional growth.

Upon arriving at Duke University School of Medicine, Sarah was eager to embark on her academic journey. Enthusiastic about contributing to the medical field, she dedicates a few days a week to volunteer at Duke University Hospital, drawing upon her previous experience at St. Anthony's. Her time volunteering not only honed her patient care skills but also nurtured her aspirations to become a surgeon. She dedicates herself to maintaining balance in her life by harmonizing her intense academic studies with her strong desire to help others.

Sarah and Luke's support for each other is clear in the daily phone calls and texts they exchange. Their profound connection shines through as they provide support, exchange news, and lend an attentive ear in moments of joy and adversity. Despite the physical distance, their connection remains steadfast, serving as a testament to the enduring power of their friendship. Through their consistent communication, Sarah and Luke exemplify the true meaning of support and companionship, proving that genuine care has no boundaries.

As winter break approaches, Sarah looks forward to the opportunity to return home for a brief respite from her studies. Despite the impending midterm exams adding to her stress and anxiety, the thought of reuniting with family and celebrating the holidays brings a sense of warmth and comfort. Sarah loves celebrating holidays with her family. They always make it special by decorating the Christmas tree together the night before and then opening presents on Christmas morning. It's something they all look forward to, and it has become a cherished tradition for them.

Christmas is a special day for Sarah's family. Her mom prepares a wonderful holiday meal with a delicious ham and all the tasty side dishes. One of Sarah's favorite traditions is baking cookies with her mom on Christmas Eve. After a well-deserved winter break, Sarah returns to school. The new semester brings with it a renewed sense of purpose and dedication as she pursues her passion for making a positive impact on the lives of patients. She focuses on fostering strong doctor-patient relationships while increasing her knowledge of the human body and healthcare practices. Dedicated to honing her skills and becoming a compassionate healthcare professional, she immerses herself in her studies.

After finishing her first year of medical school, Sarah returns home with a strong desire to apply her newly gained knowledge and skills. Devoted to her studies, Sarah perseveres and dedicates her time to volunteering at St. Anthony's, where she can make a meaningful difference in the lives of those in need. Armed with a comprehensive knowledge of medicine and a strong desire to assist others, Sarah prepares to give back to the community while gaining valuable practical experience. Her steadfast commitment and genuine passion reflect her academic endeavors and highlight her dedication to the well-being of others.

At the start of her summer holiday, Sarah and Luke catch up on the most recent happenings in their charming town. Luke invited Sarah to his house, hinting at something important he wished to discuss. The sound of tires crunching on gravel announces Sarah's arrival. As she got out of the car, the trees along the driveway rustled with a gust of wind, heightening her curiosity and excitement.

Luke met her at the door, a hesitant smile on his face. "Hey, Sarah. Come on in." She followed him inside, noting the solemn atmosphere. "What's going on, Luke? You seem… different." Settling into the living room, Luke took a deep breath before speaking. "I got some news from my parents. They want me to take over the family business sooner than expected."

Sarah's eyes widened. "I thought you had more time. What's changed?"

"My dad's health is getting worse, and it's becoming obvious that he needs to take a break. The company needs a replacement, and they believe I'm capable. But I'm not sure if I'm ready for that responsibility."

Sarah reached out, placing a reassuring hand on his arm. "Luke, you're one of the most capable people I know. If anyone can handle this, it's you."

"Thanks, Sarah. Your words mean a lot. It's not just about capability, though; I'm not sure if this is what I want."

"Tell me, Luke, what is your heart's desire? Given the opportunity, what would you pursue?"

Luke leaned back, staring at the ceiling as if the answer might appear there. "I don't know. Part of me wants to explore my opportunities at St. Anthony's. But another part of me feels obligated to stay and help my family. They've done so much for me."

"It's okay to feel torn. It's a huge decision. But whatever you decide, just know I'll support you. We're in this together, remember?"

Luke gave her a grateful smile. "Yeah, I remember. Thanks, Sarah. You always know what to say."

They spent the rest of the afternoon discussing Luke's options, weighing the pros and cons of each choice. When Sarah left, Luke felt a bit calmer, but the decision still weighed heavily on him. Later that evening, Sarah reflected on their conversation. She realized how lucky she was to have Luke by her side, always supporting her dreams, even while grappling with his own challenges.

The next morning, Sarah arrived at St. Anthony's early, her anticipation mingling with the cool morning air. She checked her reflection in the rearview mirror, taking a deep breath to steady her nerves. Today could mark a significant milestone in her journey to becoming a cardiothoracic surgeon.

Inside the hospital, she made her way to the cardiology wing, where she would meet Dr. Blake. Her mind buzzed with thoughts of the upcoming meeting, interspersed with concern for Luke and his decision.

Dr. Blake greeted her with a warm smile. "Good to see you, Sarah. How was your first year of medical school?"

They sat down, and Sarah felt at ease with Dr. Blake's approachable demeanor. "Thank you, Dr. Blake. It was challenging but incredibly rewarding." Their conversation flowed, touching on Sarah's aspirations, her volunteer experiences, and her thirst for knowledge. Dr. Blake shared insights from his own career, emphasizing the importance of resilience and adaptability in the medical field.

"Medicine demands empathy and intelligence," he remarked, his eyes gleaming with insight.

"I truly appreciate your kind words, Dr. Blake," she replied, feeling encouraged and supported in her pursuits.

Bolstered by his encouragement, Sarah left the meeting with a renewed sense of purpose. She couldn't wait to share the details with Luke.

When she met Luke again for an evening walk, the fragrance of blooming flowers filled the air—a stark contrast to his earlier somber mood. Luke seemed more optimistic, his indecision replaced by a tentative sense of clarity. "I've been thinking a lot," he admitted as they walked through the park. "Our conversation last night made me realize the importance of staying true to myself, no matter what decisions I make."

"So, have you decided?" she asked, her voice filled with anticipation.

Luke nodded, a determined look in his eyes. "I'm going to give it a shot. I'll take over the family business at the beginning of the new year, but I'm also setting up a plan to pursue my own interests. A balance, so to speak."

Sarah's heart swelled with pride. "That's a wise decision, Luke. I'm confident you'll figure it out. And when you do, I'll be right here cheering you on."

The twilight air was still and balmy as Sarah and Luke walked through the park, the tranquility a stark contrast to the whirlwind of changes in their lives. Sarah's thoughts were a jumble of excitement and determination, still electrified from her meeting with Dr. Blake. Beside her, Luke seemed more at ease, his decision to balance family duties with personal ambitions lifting a weight off his shoulders.

As they rounded a bend in the path, the rustle of leaves underfoot became the only sound between them. Sarah was about to continue their conversation when they noticed a figure standing near a bench, watching them with a piercing gaze. The stranger's presence was both unsettling and intriguing. Luke glanced at Sarah, a silent question in his eyes, before addressing the stranger. "Can we help you with something?" he asked.

The stranger, a middle-aged man with distinguished graying hair and a serious expression, moved closer. "I couldn't help but overhear. You're Sarah, right?"

Sarah's guard went up. "Yes, that's me. And you are?"

"My name is Robert," he replied, his voice calm yet urgent. "I have some vital information about Dr. Blake. It's important that you hear it."

Sarah exchanged a puzzled look with Luke before turning back to Robert. "What kind of information?"

Robert glanced around the park as if ensuring they were alone. "Dr. Blake is under investigation for malpractice. There are allegations that he's been mishandling cases at St. Anthony's," he said.

Panic surged through Sarah as she heard those words, her mind racing to disprove the unsettling claim. "What? I've met Dr. Blake. He exudes genuine compassion and skill."

"That's exactly why it's so shocking. It's best that you know now, rather than later, before you become too entangled. I suggest you proceed with caution," he advised, his tone laced with concern.

Luke stepped closer, eyes narrowed in suspicion. "Could you tell me why you're telling us this? How do you have this information?"

"I worked with Dr. Blake in the past, but I became concerned about something and left the hospital. The whole situation made me feel uneasy and uncomfortable."

Sarah contemplated Robert's words as her thoughts raced. If what he said was true, it could change everything from that moment on.

Luke, sensing her turmoil, put a reassuring hand on her shoulder and said, "Sarah, let's verify this information before jumping to conclusions."

Sarah shifted her gaze towards Luke and admitted, "You're right. I need to uncover the truth." She walked away, determined to get to the bottom of things.

Throughout the night, Sarah tossed and turned, her mind consumed by a flurry of desperate thoughts and unanswered questions. The accusations shook her resolve, despite her trusting her intuition. Understanding the situation was of utmost importance to her.

The next few days were a blur of non-stop research. Sarah and Luke worked together, combing through articles, reports, and speaking to other staff members. Luke leveraged his resources in the HR department to conduct a more in-depth investigation.

Finally, they received a message from Robert containing documents filled with unsettling details. Dr. Blake's records and testimonials from patients revealed discrepancies that alarmed them.

Looking troubled, Sarah sat down in Luke's kitchen, sharing her shock at discovering an unexpected link between someone who had inspired her and a tragic incident.

Luke wrapped his arm around her, offering a sense of comfort. "Don't worry, Sarah," he said with a comforting smile. "We'll get through this together. You can't give up on your dream just because one mentor disappoints you. You can find solace and encouragement from like-minded individuals who share your values."

His words were a balm to her wounded spirit. She knew he was right. Her journey was far from over, and she was determined to carry on, even if it meant taking a detour.

As they sat in reflective silence, Sarah made a resolution. "I'm going to talk to Dr. Blake directly. I need to hear his side of the story."

Luke nodded in agreement. "I'll be by your side."

With a newfound sense of clarity and purpose, Sarah prepared herself for the challenging conversation ahead. She understood that whatever the outcome, she needed to confront the truth.

The next day, they made plans to meet with Dr. Blake. The closer they got to his office at St. Anthony's, the more Sarah's emotions swirled in a storm of anxiety and determination. Regardless of what happened, she was prepared to confront the truth.

Dr. Blake welcomed them with his typical warm smile, but Sarah now questioned her perception of him. As she looked at Dr. Blake, she took a deep breath, her expression serious, and her voice steady as she spoke. "There's something important we really need to talk about," she said, her tone conveying the gravity of the situation.

As she voiced her concerns and presented the evidence, she watched for any signs of guilt or indignation.

Dr. Blake absorbed the information, his demeanor shifting from astonishment to calm seriousness.

Finally, he said, "Sarah, I understand your concerns. I am aware of the allegations and have been cooperating with the investigation. I assure you, my intentions have always been to help my patients. There have been some regrettable outcomes, but I've never intentionally caused harm."

"Dr. Blake, I really want to believe what you're saying," she admitted, her tone hesitant but hopeful. "But this is more than just a job—it's my entire career and future." The weight of her words hung in the air. "I can't afford any mistakes," she said firmly.

Dr. Blake nodded. "I respect that, Sarah. If you need to distance yourself from me during this investigation, I understand. But I promise you, once I clear my name, I will work even harder to regain your trust."

The conversation left Sarah with more questions than answers, but one thing was clear: she needed to carve her own path with unwavering integrity, regardless of external influences.

With Luke by her side, Sarah stepped out of the office, feeling a renewed sense of determination wash over her.

As she ventured forward on her personal journey, she relied on Luke's timeless companionship and her unshakeable resolve to achieve her dreams.

As they walked hand in hand, Luke gave her a reassuring squeeze. "Sarah," he said encouragingly, "remember, no matter what happens, you've got this. And so do I. Together, we'll find the path that leads us to our future."

With shared resolve and the strength of their friendship, Sarah and Luke faced the future, ready to embrace whatever challenges lay ahead.

As Sarah relaxed in her room, the soft evening sun cast a golden glow, lighting up her notes from the past few days. The discoveries about Dr. Blake had left her feeling conflicted, but her drive to succeed was stronger than ever.

Lost in her thoughts, a gentle chime from her laptop startled her, breaking the silence. An email notification popped up on her screen, surprising her with its unexpected sender.

Curious, she opened the email and read the subject line: "An Opportunity to Learn – Professor Evelyn Novak." She clicked on it, her eyes widening with each line she read.

Professor Novak was offering a specialized workshop on innovative cardiovascular surgery techniques and had invited Sarah to attend.

Sarah couldn't help but feel a rush of excitement as she read on. Professor Novak, a renowned heart specialist, was famous for her groundbreaking techniques in cardiovascular surgery, making her a true pioneer in the field. This invitation ignited a spark of hope amid the chaos. Sarah eagerly accepted the opportunity.

As she sent her reply to Professor Novak, her phone buzzed with a text from Luke. "Hey, I've got some exciting news. Can we meet up?"

Sarah replied, "Absolutely. See you at the park in 20 minutes."

When Sarah arrived at the park, she spotted Luke sitting on their favorite bench, his face beaming with excitement.

"Sarah, you won't believe what I've discovered," he began, his voice brimming with excitement.

"During my research on the documents submitted by Robert, I found a potential piece of evidence that could clear Dr. Blake of any wrongdoing."

Sarah's eyes flickered with relief. "That's incredible, Luke! Tell me more."

"In five surgical procedures, Robert played a crucial role in ensuring that the instruments were sterilized and prepared for use. Robert is at fault. Dr. Blake, as the lead surgeon, bears responsibility for the incident in the operating room, but Robert's actions were the root cause."

Sarah nodded, feeling relieved. "Robert's decision to leave the hospital makes sense now. His guilt made it difficult for him to face Dr. Blake daily. He made an unjust accusation, claiming Dr. Blake's incompetence."

Just as they were reveling in their newfound discovery, Sarah's phone buzzed with a call from the hospital.

Her brow furrowed as she answered. "Hello, this is Sarah."

She recognized the voice on the other end of the line as Cindy, a nurse from St. Anthony's, and sensed the urgency in her tone. "We need you to come to the hospital as soon as possible. Something strange is happening here, and we think you can help."

Sarah exchanged a worried glance with Luke. "I'll be right there, Cindy."

Luke stood up, ready to accompany her. "Let's go."

When they arrived at the hospital, a flurry of activity greeted them. Staff members were talking in hushed tones, and there was a palpable sense of unease in the air. Cindy met them at the entrance, her expression grim.

"What's going on, Cindy?" Sarah asked, keeping her voice steady.

"There have been a series of unexplained incidents," Cindy replied, her voice filled with unease. "Equipment malfunctions, misplaced patient records, and, to make matters worse, a missing medication shipment. It feels like someone is deliberately causing chaos in the hospital. Do you have any idea who could be responsible?"

Her face showed her frustration. Shaking her head, Cindy expressed her disbelief with a gesture. Her voice, filled with resolve and a slight wavering, said, "Not yet," her eyes reflecting her conflicted emotions. But I had confidence in her investigative skills, hoping she could lend us a hand in unraveling the mystery. "Let's work together to resolve this," she said confidently. Doggedly, she added, "We're in this together."

They began their investigation, starting with the malfunctioning equipment in the cardiology wing. Sarah examined the machines, noting anything out of the ordinary. Meanwhile, Luke spoke with staff members, researching and piecing together a timeline of events. Their efforts led them to the hospital's supply room, where they found evidence of tampering.

Sarah's heart pounded as she realized the severity of the situation. "Someone is definitely sabotaging us," she said firmly. "We need to find out who and why." Luke nodded, his expression resolute. "Let's keep digging. We'll find the truth."

As the night wore on, their investigation uncovered a network of compromised systems and suspicious activities. They contacted the hospital's IT department for further help, hoping to trace the source of the disruptions.

Sarah and Luke, exhausted but determined, made their way back to Sarah's house to regroup. They sat in her living room, reviewing their findings and contemplating their next steps.

"It's clear that someone has access to sensitive areas of the hospital," Sarah said, her voice tinged with frustration. "We need to figure out their motive." Luke leaned back, his brow furrowed in thought. "And we need to do it quickly before they cause any more damage."

Just then, Sarah's inbox pinged with yet another email notification, interrupting her train of thought. As she opened it, a message from Professor Novak greeted her: "Looking forward to meeting you at the workshop. P.S. Be prepared for a few surprises."

"From the looks of it, my new mentor has some surprising things lined up for me," Sarah said.

Luke grinned. "Well, it seems like we're full of surprises these days."

Sarah and Luke were aware their journey was still far from complete as they readied themselves to confront the upcoming challenges. Despite their shared determination, a lurking unease crept through their bones as they prepared to face the mysteries of St. Anthony's, unsure of what awaited them.

As Sarah and Luke made their way to St. Anthony's Hospital the next morning, Sarah could feel a surge of anticipation building inside her. They were both tired and worn out from the events of the past few days, but their determination continued to fuel them. Sarah's mind struggled to process the perplexing incidents at the hospital and the anticipation of the workshop with Professor Novak. The lingering promise of surprises filled her mind, enticing her curiosity.

Once at the hospital, their priority was going to Dr. Blake's office to discuss the act of sabotage.

Despite his exhaustion, Dr. Blake still found the strength to greet them with a smile.

"Sarah, Luke, I appreciate your efforts. I trust you've made some progress?" Dr. Blake asked, his eyes betraying his underlying concern.

"We have," Sarah replied, exchanging a glance with Luke. "However, much remains to be discovered. Someone with inside knowledge is behind this, and we need to dig deeper." Dr. Blake nodded, his expression serious. "I understand. Keep me informed of any new developments. I'll offer any help that I can."

As they left the office, Sarah's phone buzzed with a text message from Professor Novak: "Meet me in the staff lounge. There's something I need to share."

Intrigued, Sarah and Luke made their way to the lounge, where Professor Novak was waiting. She greeted them with a warm smile, but her eyes held a hint of something deeper, something unresolved. "Thank you for coming," she began, her tone slightly strained. "There's something you should know regarding the incidents at St. Anthony's."

Sarah and Luke listened as Professor Novak recounted her story. "Years ago, I worked at this hospital. During that time, I was close with a colleague named Dr. Henry Graves. He was an exceptional surgeon but had unconventional methods."

Professor Novak hesitated, her voice lowering. "Dr. Graves was involved in some... ethically questionable practices. I distanced myself from him, but it seems his influence has lingered. I suspect someone loyal to him may be behind these recent incidents."

Luke furrowed his brow. "Any leads on this person?" he asked.

Professor Novak shook her head. "None. The old records may contain answers. A hidden room in the basement holds the records."

Sarah's eyes widened. "A hidden room? How do we access it?"

Professor Novak handed them a small, ornate key. "This key will unlock the door. Be careful."

With renewed determination, Sarah and Luke ventured into the basement. The air grew cooler as they descended, the fluorescent lights flickering as if in trepidation. They followed Professor Novak's directions to a nondescript storage room and found a disguised door along its back wall.

Sarah inserted the key, and with an audible click, the door creaked open to reveal a dusty room filled with old files and medical records. They began sifting through the documents, the air thick with the musty scent of aged paper.

After an hour of searching, Sarah stumbled upon a file marked "Dr. Henry Graves - Confidential."

"Luke, look at this!" she called out, her voice tinged with excitement. They opened the file together, scanning the contents. It contained detailed notes on controversial experiments and a list of names, including former patients and staff members who had departed from St. Anthony's.

"This is disturbing," Luke muttered, frowning as he read. "But it might be exactly what we need to pinpoint the saboteur."

Their day continued with further investigation, involving more staff and uncovering additional layers of the hospital's inner workings. Luke's involvement in the environmental program took on a dual purpose; not only was he passionate about making a difference, but he also aspired to be there for Sarah, helping her navigate the uncertainty of the hospital's situation.

Later that evening, they sat in Sarah's living room, their laptops open and papers spread across the coffee table. Luke looked up from his notes, his eyes full of contemplation.

"Sarah, I've been thinking. I should take on a more active role in the environmental program while we continue this investigation. It could help me clear my mind and also give us another angle to approach this from."

As her eyes sparkled with pride, Sarah couldn't help but smile. "That is a good idea, Luke. You've always been passionate about the environment, and it might be the perfect balance you need."

Luke's smile matched hers. "I'll reach out to the program heads and see how I can get more involved. Meanwhile, we keep pushing forward here."

Their conversation veered into hopeful territories, discussing potential futures and the impact they wanted to make. Sarah felt an intense camaraderie that extended beyond friendship.

The next morning, Sarah woke with a renewed sense of purpose. She had another meeting with Professor Novak, who promised further insights into the mysteries of St. Anthony's. She arrived at Professor Novak's office with a determined stride, ready to tackle whatever came next.

As she entered, Professor Novak greeted her with a smile. "Good to see you, Sarah. Any updates on the investigation?"

"We've made some significant discoveries, but we're at a crossroads. I was hoping you could offer some guidance," Sarah said.

She presented the scanned files discovered by her and Luke from the basement. Professor Novak analyzed the documents, her expression reflecting deep contemplation.

"This is definitely concerning. However, every challenge brings an opportunity for growth and learning. Let's collaborate to solve this puzzle."

With a shared determination, Sarah and Professor Novak delved into the complexities of the evidence, committed to uncovering the truth and preserving St. Anthony's integrity. Sarah firmly believed she was prepared to confront whatever lay ahead, with the support of her steadfast friends and newfound mentors.

Sarah and Luke moved through the bustling hospital corridors with a sense of urgency. The need to uncover the truth behind the sabotage, which had put countless lives at risk, propelled each step they took. The power outage served as a grim reminder of the stakes, and they were determined to prevent further harm by stopping the saboteur.

As they reached the maintenance area, Sarah's mind was a swirl of thoughts. "Who is behind this?" she wondered. Luke's environmental initiative had provided crucial links, tracing discrepancies back to the maintenance crew.

"We must confront and expose them now," Luke said.

They found themselves in the break room for the maintenance staff, where a few workers stood gathered. Sarah scanned the room, her eyes landing on an older man sitting in the corner. His name was Marcus, a long-time employee who had always kept to himself.

Luke nudged Sarah, whispering, "That's him. The records show he has a past connection with Dr. Henry Graves."

Sarah approached Marcus, her heart pounding. "Marcus, we need to talk," she said, her voice steady but firm.

Marcus looked up, a flicker of something unreadable in his eyes, before he nodded and stood. Sarah and Luke led him to a secluded part of the hospital where they could speak in private. As soon as the door closed behind them, Marcus's demeanor changed. He looked wary and anxious, his hands fidgeting.

"Marcus," Sarah started softly, "we are aware of your association with Dr. Henry Graves, and we're also aware of the recent incidents at the hospital. We need you to tell us the truth."

Marcus's eyes darted between Sarah and Luke before he took a deep breath. "I never meant for it to reach this point," he confessed, his voice quivering. "I was just... doing what Dr. Graves asked of me."

Luke stepped forward, his expression stern. "What did he ask you to do, Marcus?"

Marcus's shoulders slumped, defeated. "He wanted me to create disruptions, make it look like the hospital was failing in its duties. He said it was necessary to expose the weaknesses in the system. I didn't realize how dangerous it would become."

Before Sarah could respond, Marcus dashed toward the door. "Stop!" she called out, but it was too late. Marcus ran down the hallway, pushing past staff and patients alike. Sarah and Luke chased after him, their hearts racing.

The chase led them through a maze of corridors and stairwells, finally reaching the hospital's waste disposal area. Marcus stumbled, knocking over bins and creating a chaotic mess. As he tried to climb over a locked gate, Luke tackled him to the ground.

"It's over, Marcus," Luke said, his voice filled with a mix of relief and frustration. "You need to face the consequences of your actions."

As they restrained Marcus and called for security, Luke noticed something unusual among the scattered waste disposal reports. He picked up a crumpled piece of paper detailing discrepancies in waste disposal methods that connected to the sabotage.

"Sarah, look at this," Luke said, handing her the paper. "These records show unauthorized changes in waste handling, matching the incidents we've been investigating."

Sarah's eyes widened as she read through the report. "This is the break we needed. We have clear evidence now."

They walked together toward the hospital administration office, ready to present their findings and bring the saboteur to justice.

As the sun set, casting a golden glow over St. Anthony's, Sarah felt a sense of closure settling in. The trials they had faced had only strengthened their resolve and deepened their bond.

With their timeless friendship and newfound allies, Sarah and Luke knew they would continue to overcome any obstacle in their path. They were ready to face the future, one step at a time.

The morning light trickled through the hospital windows as Sarah and Luke made their way to the cafeteria. The weight of recent events still lingered, but a sense of cautious optimism remained. With Marcus's confession and the damning evidence they had uncovered, the pieces were finally falling into place. They just needed to keep pushing forward.

Over coffee, they reviewed their plans for the day.

"We need to ensure that the administration acts on our findings," Sarah said, her voice steadfast. "We can't let Marcus take the fall alone. Accountability for everyone involved is necessary."

Luke nodded, his eyes filled with resolve. "Agreed. I also think we should monitor the environmental protocols. Other underlying issues may still be hidden."

Just as they finished their discussion, Sarah's phone chimed with an email notification. She opened it to find a message from Dr. Henry Graves requesting an urgent meeting. Her heart sank; the turmoil surrounding Dr. Graves had been a source of constant tension.

"Dr. Graves wants to meet," Sarah said, showing the message to Luke. "I have a sense that this won't be a straightforward conversation."

Luke reached out with a gentle squeeze of her hand. "Whatever happens, just remember you're doing this for the right reasons. Integrity matters more than anything."

With Luke's encouragement, Sarah took a deep breath and headed to Dr. Graves' office. As she entered, his face appeared solemn. He gestured for her to sit, and she realized the weight of the moment.

"Sarah," Dr. Graves began, his voice heavy with emotion, "I've heard about the evidence you and Luke uncovered. I would like to clarify that my intentions were never to be detrimental to anyone."

Sarah's mind raced. She wanted to believe Dr. Graves, but the evidence was damning. "Dr. Graves, the findings are serious. Unauthorized procedures, discrepancies in environmental protocols— it's more than just oversight."

Dr. Graves' expression tightened. "I know it looks bad, but there were justifications for my choices. Medical necessity, urgency—all factors influenced my actions."

Sarah was conflicted, caught between her loyalty to St. Anthony's and her unwavering commitment to ethical practices. "Dr. Graves, it is crucial that patients are fully aware of the potential risks," she emphasized.

He sighed, running a hand through his hair. "You're right, Sarah. I should have communicated better. I should have been more transparent. But I didn't want to worry them unnecessarily."

She looked at him, the conflict clear in her eyes. "I have to choose integrity, Dr. Graves. The truth needs to come out. Patients' trust in us is paramount."

Dr. Graves nodded, accepting. "I understand, Sarah. Do what you must. I'll accept the consequences of my actions."

Upon exiting his office, a blend of emotions overwhelmed Sarah. She was filled with a deep resolve to uphold her principles.

As she saw Luke waiting for her outside, his encouraging smile lifted her spirits.

Luke's eagerness about the outcome of her meeting with Dr. Graves was clear in his tone, which held a delicate balance of curiosity and concern. "How did it go with Dr. Graves?" he asked, his eyes searching for clues. "Did he confess to his role in the sabotage?" Leaning closer, he held his breath, eager to hear the response that hung in the air.

In a solemn voice, Sarah said, "Dr. Graves apologized for masterminding the entire sabotage. He showed sincere regret and is ready to be held accountable."

As Luke listened, his mind became consumed with the gravity of the situation and the potential consequences that Dr. Graves' admission could bring. He grappled with the enduring complexities.

Luke's day took an unexpected turn when he received a call from the organizers of the Worldwide Sustainable Healthcare Conference. His environmental initiative had left a powerful impression on them, prompting their request for him to address the audience and share the specifics of his influential work.

"Sarah! I've been invited to speak at the international conference on sustainable healthcare!" Luke exclaimed with a mix of excitement and pride.

Sarah's face lit up with joy. "Luke, that's incredible! You've worked so hard for this. It's well-deserved recognition."

Luke's enthusiasm was infectious. "It's a tremendous opportunity, not just for me, but also to raise awareness about how sustainability and healthcare can go hand in hand. Let's make sure St. Anthony's leads the way."

As they talked, brainstorming ideas for Luke's presentation, the mood lightened. The trials they had faced had strengthened their bond, and now they were looking at a horizon filled with possibilities.

The next few weeks passed in a blur of activity. Sarah continued her work in the cardiology wing, devoting her attention to patient care. She also took immediate action to address the results of the investigation. Meanwhile, Luke prepared for his conference, balancing his new commitments with his ongoing environmental initiatives at the hospital.

Finally, the day of the international conference arrived. Luke stood on the grand stage, his heart pounding with a mix of nerves and excitement. Influential figures from the healthcare and environmental sectors were all eager to hear his insights.

He took a deep breath and began, "Good morning, everyone. Today, I want to talk about an intersection that is often overlooked—how sustainable practices can improve healthcare outcomes."

His passion and knowledge captivated the audience, drawing them into his vision of a future where hospitals were not just centers of healing, but also hubs of environmental stewardship. As he spoke, he highlighted the efforts at St. Anthony's, using their challenges and triumphs as a case study.

Luke recounted his experiences at St. Anthony's, detailing the obstacles he encountered, such as sabotage, environmental lapses, and ethical dilemmas. Yet, through resilience and collaboration, he found that integrity and sustainability can coexist, resulting in improved care quality.

At the end of his speech, the audience erupted into applause, validating his hard work and dedication. Humbled by the worldwide implications, he exited the stage.

Sarah met him backstage, her eyes gleaming with pride after the conference. "Luke," she said, her voice filled with genuine admiration, "you were absolutely amazing. Your message resonates with so many people. I'm so proud of you."

Luke smiled, pulling her into a tight hug. "Thank you, Sarah. I couldn't have done it without your support. We make a successful team, don't we?"

Sarah nodded, filled with gratitude for their friendship. "Absolutely. And together, we can face whatever challenges come our way."

With their spirits high and their resolve even stronger, Sarah and Luke knew their journey was far from over. They would continue to navigate the complexities of their careers, always guided by the principles of integrity, sustainability, and the power of timeless friendship.

Chapter 6

Finding Resilience in Loss
Coping with Grief and Seeking Help

Sarah's heart races with excitement as she envisions applying for residency at St. Anthony's. The vibrant colors of the bustling hospital corridors fill her eyes, while urgent footsteps and beeping monitors fill her ears. The distinct scent of antiseptic lingers in the air, heightening her anticipation. Sarah can feel Dr. Blake's palpable energy and knowledge igniting a fire within her to learn and grow under his guidance.

A deep sense of gratitude engulfs Sarah as she sits in muted reflection. Vibrant memories of his unwavering support and valuable guidance during her time at Duke flood her thoughts. As she thinks about her future, she hopes to further her medical education with the guidance of this respected mentor. The recent dismissal of the malicious malpractice lawsuit against Dr. Blake fills her with immense joy and a profound sense of relief.

Sarah's entire world crumbled when Luke delivered a heart-wrenching call on a cold winter day. His voice stutters when she answers the phone. "Sarah, I… I need to tell you something about your parents." He swallows the lump in his throat and questions his own thoughts on how to tell her.

Concern fills her voice. "What is it, Luke?" she asks.

With tears rolling down his cheeks, he musters the strength to speak. "I am so sorry. Your parents have been involved in a fatal accident."

A wave of shock sweeps over her, rendering her motionless in a moment of indescribable sorrow.

Sarah gasps for air, her chest heaving as if she had been running for miles. The room seems to spin around her as she struggles to catch her breath. "Luke," her voice trembling, "this... this can't be true."

The weight of disbelief hangs heavy in the air, making it difficult for her to comprehend what she has just heard. The room feels suffocating, as if the walls are closing in on her, amplifying her sense of unease.

Luke offers his support with a voice filled with empathy. "How can I help you with your flight back home? I'll be at the airport to pick you up as soon as you arrive."

"Thank you, Luke. I need to call the airlines and see what flights are available. I will call you back with the details as soon as I have them."

The unexpected news shatters Sarah's tranquil day, jolting her senses and leaving her heart pounding. As the weight of the sudden loss washes over her, she struggles to process the unfathomable pain that now defines her existence. With tears in her eyes, she books her flight home, overwhelmed by grief. With sorrow in the air, she begins the daunting task of arranging her parents' funeral, forever changing her life.

Overwhelmed with grief and disbelief, she feels adrift after the unexpected deaths of her parents. She struggles to accept the painful reality that her parents are gone, realizing she will never hear their laughter or see them again. Memories of happier times flood her mind, with their love and support echoing in her heart.

Sarah finds comfort in the memories of her parents' love, which helps her cope with the emotional pain of their tragic death.

Amid grief, Luke stands with Sarah, providing solace with his reassuring touch in the dim room. The faint scent of lilies fills the air, mingling with the sound of soft sobs and the hushed whispers of condolences. Together, they lean on each other, finding strength in their intertwined fingers as they bid farewell to Sarah's beloved parents. Sarah's friends and colleagues from St. Anthony's attend her parents' funeral to show support and offer condolences.

In the somber setting, their sincere presence is proof of the deep bonds formed from shared encounters and caring for one another. The community shows their unity and friendship by offering kind words and comfort during a difficult time.

Their presence brings Sarah solace, assuring her she isn't alone in her grief. They stand beside her, creating a comforting atmosphere of love and support throughout this challenging time. With a warm and comforting presence, Dr. Blake approaches Sarah after the funeral to offer his sincere condolences and unwavering support.

With Sarah's final year approaching, her loss burdens her heart, yet Dr. Blake's kindness and understanding are a beacon in her darkest moments.

His genuine care and willingness to listen and support show his professionalism and compassion. Sarah feels hopeful and supported when Dr. Blake offers his help at a vulnerable time in her life.

Sarah's voice cracks with emotion as she implores Dr. Blake for help with her residency program application, tears welling up in her eyes.

Dr. Blake embraces her with open arms, ensuring her of his support and help. His words of encouragement motivate her as he says, "Your commitment to your career goals is impressive. Call me when you can talk more in my office before you head to campus."

"Thank you," she expresses, her voice filled with sincere appreciation. "I'll contact you as soon as I can find a free moment."

Sarah's determination burns bright as she sets her sights on returning to medical school and becoming a surgeon. She shows her dedication by volunteering at St. Anthony's. The primary focus in the third year is to develop future medical leaders through an immersive exploration of biomedical research. Sarah is in the final stages of her rotations, engrossed in a flurry of activities that require her complete focus and commitment.

Through the scent of late-night coffee and the hum of her laptop, she immerses herself in her studies. Her achievements give her a strong sense of satisfaction and drive to conquer obstacles and succeed.

Determined to finish the year and reunite with Luke serves as a beacon of hope. Luke's role in her life goes beyond being a mere support system. With his steady presence and unwavering devotion, Sarah finds the strength to push through challenges and hurdles. Despite the hardships, she finds solace in the thought of reuniting with Luke and confronting whatever obstacles may cross her path.

Luke is at a pivotal moment in his life, torn between his flourishing career at St. Anthony's and the chance to lead his family's business. He's struggling to juggle both his current success and an alternative path.

He wrestles with the ethical implications for both companies; he ponders he consequences of his choice on his professional duties. Luke feels torn between his commitment to the hospital and the exciting opportunities in his family's business.

Luke dials Sarah's number, his concern clear in his voice as he checks in on her since her return to school. As they speak, Sarah's overwhelmed tone is unmistakable. Her studies are proving to be more demanding than she had expected. Sarah's usual laser-sharp focus seems to have wavered, drifting away from where it should be.

Luke supports Sarah by listening and offering encouragement during the chaotic time in school, determined to help her regain her focus. He asks, "Sarah, have you considered taking a break this summer before your last year at Duke to refresh and recharge?"

Sarah exhales, filled with emotion. "Luke, I've also been thinking about that. Maybe a break is exactly what I need for my final year challenges. However, volunteering at the hospital fills my days with joy and purpose, and leaving for a break may not be that simple," she says. Luke replies, "You can take a break without venturing too far from St. Anthony's. Your well-being must prioritize self-care, especially before such a critical year ahead. Let's brainstorm some ideas about how you can make it work."

Sarah's voice brightens as she replies, "Oh, Luke! I have confidence in your insight and trust you can help me uncover a balanced solution to my dilemma."

Luke feels comforted as he can bring solace to Sarah. "I have an upcoming meeting that I must attend in a few minutes. Take care of yourself, and we will talk soon."

Upon ending the call, Sarah feels a deep sense of comfort. Luke possesses a remarkable ability to comfort her and uplift her life. She can now concentrate on her studies and tackle the rest of this year with tenacity.

Entering the cafeteria, she spots Luke already seated at a table, awaiting her arrival. Their gazes connect, and Luke's face radiates warmth and excitement. "I'm glad we have a moment to chat," he says.

"Likewise, Luke! How has your morning been?" Sarah mirrors his enthusiasm.

Luke's smile widens, brimming with eagerness to share. "I received fantastic news today! St. Anthony's has offered me a full-time role as the assistant HR director."

"That's amazing news!" Sarah replies, her eyes lighting up with joy.

She then expresses her own thoughts about her upcoming journey. "Luke, I'll be heading to Duke in three weeks. I'm going to miss you so much."

"I will miss you too, Sarah," Luke says, his voice softening with emotion.

"But I promise you," he adds with conviction, "time at Duke will fly by just as quickly as it did at Johns Hopkins."

His words ease the uncertainty Sarah has been feeling. Luke's unwavering support reassures her that they can navigate the changes ahead, their bond stronger than any distance or challenge they may face.

Chapter 7

Reflections - Prioritizing Preparations for the Future

Seated at her desk, Sarah basked in the gentle sunlight pouring in through the window, enveloping the papers strewn in front of her with a comforting warmth.

In recent years, Sarah had experienced a series of events—medical duties, losing her parents, and investigations with Luke. Amidst the struggles, she embraced a sense of fulfillment and personal growth.

As she immersed herself in a peaceful moment of self-reflection, an email notification grabbed her attention. Opening the email, her eyes grew wide as she read the subject line: "Invitation to Publish - Ethical Challenges."
The email was from Dr. Evelyn Chamberlain, a respected editor of a prestigious medical journal. As she read the message, excitement and apprehension mingled in her mind.

Dr. Chamberlain's email was a call to share her unique experiences dealing with ethical dilemmas and the recent challenges at St. Anthony's. The editor believed that Sarah's insights could provide valuable lessons for the broader medical community. It provided a chance to underscore the value of integrity and transparency and to illuminate the difficulties they had experienced.

Sarah leaned back in her chair, fingers tapping on the desk. The chance to author a paper was both thrilling and daunting. Her mind raced with potential themes and case studies, actual stories from the trenches that had the potential to resonate with fellow practitioners. But where would she find the time amidst her already packed schedule?

As if in answer, her phone buzzed with a message from Luke: "Need to talk. Important news. Meet me at the park."

A smile tugged at the corners of Sarah's mouth. She gathered her things and rushed out, eager to hear what had Luke so animated. The park had become their sanctuary, a place to decompress and share their victories and concerns. As she approached their usual bench, she saw Luke pacing, his expression a blend of excitement and determination.

"Luke! What's the news?" she said as she got closer.

Luke turned, his face lighting up at the sight of her. "Sarah, a journalist contacted me. She's researching hospital sustainability and heard about our environmental initiatives at St. Anthony's. Her angle is to expose the sabotage and highlight how it affects both patient care and environmental standards."

Sarah's eyes widened. "That's huge, Luke. This has the possibility of attracting national attention to the challenges we've been dealing with."

Luke nodded, his gaze intense. "That's my point. But it needs to be finessed. I don't want the exposure to backfire on the hospital or our careers."

They sat on the bench, the gravity of the situation sinking in. The possibility of widespread publicity had the potential to spur action and result in systemic changes, but it also presented risks. Sarah thought about Dr. Chamberlain's invitation and the power of words to affect change and protect the integrity of their profession.

"I've received an invitation to publish a paper on our experiences," Sarah said, searching Luke's eyes for his reaction. "It could complement the journalist's story, offering an insider's perspective on the ethical challenges we faced."

Luke smiled, a look of admiration passing over his features. "That's fantastic, Sarah. Your voice holds the power to make a difference. Let's not only fix St. Anthony's issues, but also set a precedent for other hospitals."

They spent the next few hours brainstorming together, outlining key points for Sarah's paper and discussing the potential impact of Luke's interview with the journalist. They knew they had to be strategic, presenting their findings in a way that highlighted the need for transparency and reform without undermining the hospital's reputation.

As the evening shadows lengthened, they wrapped up their discussion, a sense of purpose guiding them forward. Sarah would begin drafting her paper, detailing the ethical dilemmas and investigative hurdles they had overcome. Luke would prepare for his conversation with the journalist, ensuring he presented their story with honesty and clarity.

The following weeks were a blur of activity. Between patient rounds, Sarah worked on her paper, weaving in anecdotes, data, and reflections. She reached out to Dr. Rivera and other colleagues for input, ensuring her arguments were robust and well-supported. Luke, meanwhile, coordinated with the journalist, providing detailed information and arranging interviews with key staff members who could corroborate their findings.

The day came when Sarah submitted her manuscript to the journal, her heart pounding with anticipation. The following week was when they scheduled Luke's interview, and the sense of shared destiny between them had never been stronger. They had navigated through personal and professional trials, their friendship a pillar of strength and resilience.

One crisp morning, as they sat by the hospital garden, enjoying a rare moment of tranquility, Sarah's phone buzzed with an email notification. She held her breath as she opened it, reading Dr. Chamberlain's response. As her eyes scanned the lines, a smile spread across her face.

"It's accepted," she said, her voice tinged with both disbelief and satisfaction. "Dr. Chamberlain wants to publish my paper."

Luke's face broke into a wide grin. "That's amazing, Sarah! Your hard work is paying off. This is just the beginning."

As they celebrated this milestone, they knew their journey was far from over. With Sarah's paper set to make waves in the medical community and Luke's impending interview poised to expose the sabotage, they were ready to face whatever challenges lay ahead. United by their timeless friendship and driven by a shared commitment to integrity and excellence, they embraced the future with renewed hope and determination.

Chapter 8

Seizing Opportunities
A New Dawn for Change

Sarah and Luke walked into the hospital garden, illuminated by the morning sun.

Sarah's paper being accepted for publication marked a significant triumph, yet they knew they had many more hurdles to overcome in their ongoing journey. Around them, the hospital hummed with lively discussions and fresh obstacles waiting to be tackled.

"I still can't believe it, Luke," Sarah said, her voice a mix of pride and incredulity. "Our experiences, our struggles—now shared with so many more people."

Luke smiled, his eyes filled with pride for his friend. "Sarah, you've worked hard for this. And this is only the start."

After a moment of silence, Luke spoke up, saying, "There's something I need to share with you."

Sarah turned to him, curious. "What is it?"

Luke pulled out his phone and opened an email. "I got a message from Clara Evans—an influential investor who's been following our progress with the environmental initiative. She's seen the potential of our work at St. Anthony's and wants to meet. She's offering significant support—financial and otherwise."

Sarah's eyes widened. "Clara Evans? She's a big deal, Luke. The project could undergo a significant transformation."

He nodded, brimming with eagerness. "Exactly. She's flying in next week to discuss the details. This has the potential to bring the resources and attention we need to scale our initiatives and make a real impact."

Their conversation flowed with possibilities as they envisioned a future where sustainable practices integrate into healthcare, improving patient outcomes and environmental footprints. They explored innovative approaches, potential partnerships, and ways to leverage this newfound support to drive meaningful change.

As their day unfolded, Sarah and Luke juggled their responsibilities at the hospital with preparations for the upcoming meeting. Luke drafted a comprehensive proposal outlining their achievements, ongoing projects, and future aspirations. They used every available moment to enhance their strategy, ensuring they were prepared to make the most of the opportunity Clara Evans' support provided.

The week passed in a blur of activity, and finally, the day of the meeting arrived. Luke and Sarah waited in the hospital's administrative boardroom, the polished wooden table reflecting their anxious faces. They had rehearsed their presentation, each determined to convey the importance of their work and the potential positive influence it might bring about.

A knock on the door broke the silence, and Clara Evans entered, her presence commanding and poised. Her impeccable outfit exuded an air of confidence and intelligence. Sarah and Luke stood to greet her, shaking hands and exchanging pleasantries before settling into their seats.

"Thank you for meeting with us, Ms. Evans," Luke began, his voice steady despite the nervous energy coursing through him. "We've been eagerly looking forward to discussing our work and the potential for collaboration."

Clara smiled, her cheeks flushed with happiness as her laughter filled the air, spreading contagious joy. "It's my pleasure. I'm impressed with what I've seen so far. Please proceed. I'm listening."

Luke took a deep breath and launched into their presentation. He talked with fervor about the environmental initiative, which strives to lower carbon footprints, enhance waste management, and incorporate sustainable practices into healthcare delivery.

Sarah supported him, describing the ethical aspects, their investigations, and their unwavering commitment to patient care and environmental integrity.

Clara focused, her gaze sharp and thoughtful. When they finished, a thoughtful silence hung in the room, punctuated only by the rustling of papers as Clara reviewed the proposal.

"This is impressive," Clara finally said, her tone appreciative. "Your dedication and vision are exactly what the industry needs. I'm committed to helping you turn these plans into reality."

Relief and excitement washed over Sarah and Luke. "Thank you, Ms. Evans," Sarah said. "Your support means everything to us. This initiative can set a new standard for healthcare institutions everywhere."

Clara nodded. "I agree. And please, call me Clara. I see a lot of potential here, and I'm eager to get started. Let's discuss the next steps and how we can best allocate resources to ensure maximum impact."

The meeting continued with detailed discussions on funding, project timelines, and potential partnerships. Clara's expertise and strategic insights were invaluable, providing clarity and direction as they mapped out the path forward.

As the session was ending, Clara stood up and reached out her hand. "I'm looking forward to the successful things we can achieve together, Sarah and Luke. My team will draft the partnership agreements, and we can soon proceed with the formalization of all the details."

They shook hands, a sense of accomplishment and anticipation filling the room. "Thank you, Clara," Luke said, his voice filled with gratitude. "This is the start of something big."

As they exited the boardroom, Sarah and Luke experienced a sense of relief, their optimism heightened by the prospect of support and validation. They had taken another significant step toward their goals, and the future looked brighter than ever.

"We did it, Luke," Sarah said, a beaming smile lighting up her face. "This is going to change everything."

Luke nodded, his eyes reflecting the same enthusiasm. "Yes, it will. Together, we're going to make a real difference."

Chapter 9

Embracing the Unknown
A Path of Love and Resilience

As Sarah and Luke continued their daily rounds and responsibilities at St. Anthony's, life had a way of presenting new challenges and opportunities in tandem. The news of Clara Evans' support had filled them with hope and optimism, but fate had other plans in store.

Luke faced a crisis of his own. His phone buzzed with a message from his mother, the words causing his heart to pound. In a rush to the ICU, he located his father, John, being prepped for emergency surgery. The aneurysm in his father's aorta had enlarged to a dangerous point, and immediate intervention was required.

Sarah reached the intensive care unit, showing her concern. "Luke," her voice choked with tears, "I'm so sorry," she said, her eyes welling up with sorrow. "How is he?" Her voice trembled, her eyes welling up with tears, dreading the answer that would confirm her worst fears.

"Dr. Blake says it's critical, Sarah," Luke replied, his voice filled with sorrow, the weight of the news making his shoulders slump and his eyes well up with tears. "My heart pounds as uncertainty grips me, leaving me paralyzed in a sea of indecision."

With a delicate touch, Sarah held his hand, her fingers trembling as tears welled up in her eyes. "I know Dr. Blake will go above and beyond," she said, with a radiant smile spreading across her face.

Sarah's hands trembled as she pressed them against the observation room window, her eyes filled with desperation, praying that Dr. Blake's delicate procedure on John's heart would save his life.

Every moment brimmed with electric anticipation, each second bursting with the potential for a triumphant victory that would make John's heart soar.

As the surgery progressed, Sarah's thoughts drifted to Luke for a moment, and a wave of melancholy washed over her, causing tears to well up in her eyes. She grasped how crucial his family was to him and the burden he bore from the impending responsibility of the family business. Right now, the primary concern was to save John's life.

Hours later, the surgeon emerged from the operating room, his face pale and beads of sweat glistening on his forehead, relieved that the surgery was successful. Sarah breathed a sigh of relief as she left the observation room. She spotted Luke in the waiting room, his eyes wide with terror as he clutched onto the armrest of the chair. The moment their eyes met, she offered him a reassuring smile.

With a calm voice, she reassured Luke that his father's surgery was complete and successful. "He is in stable condition, but he will need constant monitoring and extensive help," she said.

Luke let out a deep exhale, feeling a sense of relief flood through his body. "I am grateful, Sarah. We need your input for decision-making."

In the days that followed, Luke's father began his slow journey to recovery. Luke spent countless hours at his bedside, grappling with the reality of stepping up to take over the family business.

One evening, as Sarah and Luke sat by John's bedside, the beeping of the monitors as a backdrop to their thoughts, Luke finally voiced his inner turmoil. "Sarah, I am uncertain about my ability to accomplish this. The business, my dad's recovery... it's all so overwhelming."

Sarah looked at him, her eyes filled with empathy. "Luke, you've always been strong. You have all the tools to succeed, and you don't have to do it alone. Lean on your family, your friends. Lean on me," she said.

Luke's gaze softened. "I don't want to disappoint anyone," he said.

"You won't," Sarah assured him. "We'll navigate this together. And remember, accepting help doesn't make you weak—it's a sign of strength."

Luke nodded, a newfound resolve settling within him. Together, they would face these challenges, drawing strength from their unbreakable bond and the unwavering support they provided each other.

Luke sat by his father's bedside, the dim light of the hospital room casting gentle shadows on the walls. John's breathing was steady, a sign of his gradual recovery. The room was silent except for the rhythmic beeping of the monitors and the occasional murmur from the corridor.

Sarah had left moments earlier to check on her patients, leaving Luke alone with his thoughts.

As Luke watched his father rest, a mix of emotions surged within him—relief, gratitude, and overwhelming responsibility swirled together. The weight of the family business now appeared more overwhelming than ever.

With a quick glance, he observed the folder he had brought, realizing it contained the valuable contents his dad had always safeguarded. Despite the need for him to take action, doubt continued to gnaw at him.

Lost in thought, Luke didn't notice his mother's presence until she touched his shoulder. "Luke," she whispered, her eyes filled with warmth and an unspoken depth of emotion, "there's something you should understand."

He looked up, concern etching his features. "Mom? What is it?" he said.

She took a deep breath, pulling a chair closer to sit beside him. "Your father and I have kept a secret from you for many years. It was something we thought would shield you, but now I realize you deserve to be aware of the truth."

Confusion flashed across Luke's face. "What are you talking about?" he asked.

"Before your father fully took over the business, there was a time when we were struggling," she began, her voice wavering slightly. "Your father had invested in a project that went awry. It bankrupted us."

Luke's eyes widened in shock. "Why didn't you tell me?"

"We didn't want you to worry, especially when you were younger," she explained. "But it's crucial that you are aware your father completely changed the situation. He took a failing business and brought it back to life. He made sacrifices, worked tirelessly, and made it thrive," she said.

Luke absorbed her words, a new understanding dawning on him. "So, you're saying... I can do this too?" he asked.

She nodded, a tear slipping down her cheek. "You have the same strength and determination as your father. You have what it takes to lead the business to even greater heights."

As he felt a renewed sense of purpose wash over him, Luke embraced his mother, deriving comfort and empowerment from her reassuring words. Recognizing the obstacles that awaited him, he still respected his father's legacy and decided to take on the responsibility of running the family enterprise.

When evening came, Luke made his way to Sarah's place. The heart-to-heart with his mother left Luke's mind filled with a whirlwind of thoughts. Aware of the significance of a direct conversation with Sarah, he rounded the corner near her house.

Luke arrived, knocked, and Sarah opened the door to find him with a determined look. "Come in, Luke," Sarah said with a smile.

"Sarah, we need to talk," he said, his voice steady.

She motioned for him to sit, curiosity sparking in her mind. "What's on your mind, Luke?"

He took a deep breath, gathering his thoughts. "My mother told me about a struggle my father faced when he first took over the business. It changed my perspective. Knowing that he overcame such a tremendous obstacle gives me the confidence I needed."

Sarah smiled, her eyes reflecting her support. "That's amazing, Luke. It sounds like you're ready to embrace your role fully."

Luke agreed with a nod. "I am!" His voice filled with infectious delight, as if a burst of sunshine had entered the room.

"There's another matter we need to discuss. I have so many thoughts running through my head."

Sarah's heart skipped a beat, sensing a shift in the atmosphere. "What is it?"

Luke stood up, taking her hand in his. He looked into her eyes, his gaze unwavering. "Sarah, you've been my rock through all of this. Your support, your friendship, your love—it's been everything to me."

Tears welled up in Sarah's eyes as she squeezed his hand. "Luke, you mean the world to me."

He reached into his pocket and pulled out a small velvet box, opening it to reveal a sparkling ring. "Sarah, will you marry me? Would you like to continue this journey by my side as my wife and partner?"

Overwhelmed with emotion, Sarah's face beamed with a radiant smile, her heart fluttering with delight. "Yes, Luke, yes!" she exclaimed, her eyes sparkling with joy as she embraced him tightly, unable to contain her happiness. "I am overjoyed to be your wife and partner now and for all eternity."

Luke slipped the ring onto her finger, pure happiness radiating from both of them.

Sarah was mindful of the fact that she had one more year to go before finishing medical school. She and Luke were considering postponing their wedding until after she graduated. Despite encountering many challenges, they had remained united throughout. Luke was preparing to take on the family business, striving to absorb as much knowledge as possible, while Sarah focused on completing her last year of medical school.

Sarah and Luke were ready for their next chapter, committed to their shared dreams.

Chapter 10

Embracing Change
A Vision for the Future

Luke stared at the ledger, the figures blurring together as his mind wandered. The responsibility of managing the family business had been more taxing than he had imagined. Juggling financial forecasting, employee management, and daily operations felt like a hard task. Yet, he remained resolute, fueled by the memory of his father's perseverance.

As he reminisced about his childhood, memories of accompanying his father to work flooded his mind. He recalled the feeling of importance as he settled into the chair behind his father's desk, imagining himself as the boss of the office. The presence of his father and the office ambiance sparked his fascination with business.

These experiences shaped his perception and instilled in him a sense of ambition and leadership that would guide him on his own career journey. He glanced at a picture on his desk—Sarah, radiating joy, her eyes full of encouragement. She was his anchor in this tumultuous sea of responsibilities.

As he looked at the photo, a surge of admiration filled his heart. He reflected on the depth of her ambition and the unwavering determination that propelled her towards her dream of becoming a surgeon. The challenges and hurdles Sarah had faced in the past few years only strengthened his admiration for her resilience. He was proud of her unshakable spirit and her ability to persevere in the face of adversity. He realized the depth of his feelings for Sarah and how much she meant to him as he witnessed her unwavering pursuit of her goals.

Sarah and Luke had been planning their wedding amidst their overwhelming schedules, finding solace in envisioning a future together, even as chaos reigned around them. Luke's fingers hesitated over the keypad before pressing the familiar digits of Sarah's phone number. He missed her more than he had imagined since she left for Duke.

Despite the distance between them, a sense of warmth enveloped him at the sound of her laughter, a reminder of the connection they shared. When they spoke, the miles between them seemed to fade away, replaced by the comfort of their conversation.

When Sarah's phone rang, she answered with a cheerful "Hello!" The sound of her voice brought a rush of emotions, the longing clear in his tone. "Hey Sarah, I needed to hear your voice, to feel a sense of connection. How is everything going with you?"

"Hey Luke, I'm doing okay. Thanks for calling. I'm happy to hear your voice. How are you holding up?"

"I'm hanging in there. Just staying positive and keeping busy. I miss seeing you, though. It feels like forever since we were together."

"I know," her voice was filled with understanding. "Being unable to see each other has been tough, especially considering the time we spent together. Hopefully, things will return to normal soon. How has work been treating you?"

"It's been busy, but I'm grateful to have a job during all of this. How's everything going on your end?" he asked.

"It's been a whirlwind of stress, but I'm staying positive and taking each day as it comes. Knowing that you're checking in on me brings me comfort," she said.

Luke chuckled, his laughter filling the air, and said, "Well, I'm always here for you."

"Thank you," she said, feeling a wave of appreciation wash over her. "I appreciate that. I feel lucky to have you in my life, and I'm hoping to see you soon."

Luke's response was definitive as he said, "Without a doubt. Take care of yourself and remember, I'm just a phone call away, ready to lend an ear whenever you need to talk. Talk to you soon."

"Thanks," Sarah said, her voice filled with appreciation. "You as well. Bye."

Sarah was balancing her final year in medical school with grace. Her four-year program taught her the fundamentals of medicine and patient care. To secure a strong surgical residency placement, she applied her knowledge during clinical rotations and always maintained excellent grades. Her thoughts often wandered to the upcoming wedding, and a heavy sigh escaped her lips as she imagined the absence of her late father walking her down the aisle. Tears welled up in her eyes, burdened by wedding preparations and a hectic schedule, dampening the happiness of the occasion. Yet, as she envisioned her life entwined with Luke's, a bittersweet ache settled in her chest as tears flowed from her eyes.

Back at home, Luke embraced his developing role within his family's business, displaying a resolute determination in his approach. Equipped with a strategic mindset and a well-defined vision, he was charting a course towards a brighter future for the company, with aspirations to propel it to unprecedented achievements.

By introducing innovative concepts and offering a fresh perspective, he was revitalizing the business, instilling a newfound vigor and purpose within the team. Through his wholehearted dedication and ambitious spirit, his position enabled him to steer the business towards expansion and prosperity, driven by his steadfast resolve to transcend its current limits.

He was uncertain about the upcoming board meeting and how the members would respond to his proposed direction for the company. When he entered the boardroom, his mind raced with thoughts about the upcoming meeting. He had spent countless hours preparing a comprehensive plan to steer the family business toward a more sustainable and innovative future.

Today, he would present his vision to the board members, hoping they would recognize the potential benefits and support his initiatives. However, as he sat down, he noticed the stern expression on Mr. Thompson's face, one of the most influential and traditional board members. Luke took a deep breath, ready to present his case despite the tension in the room.

"Thank you all for being here today," Luke began, projecting confidence. "I've spent the past few months reviewing our current strategies and identifying areas where we can innovate and grow, particularly in sustainable practices and new market expansions."

He presented a series of slides highlighting proposed changes, including eco-friendly product lines, new market sectors, and efficiency improvements. Most of the board members seemed interested, but Mr. Thompson's scowl deepened with every passing minute.

When he concluded his presentation, he opened the floor for questions. Mr. Thompson was the first to speak, his tone sharp. "Your proposed changes risk destabilizing our market position."

Luke expected resistance but remained steadfast. "Mr. Thompson, the market is growing. Consumers are increasingly interested in sustainable and innovative products. If we don't adapt, we risk falling behind. These changes are not just necessary; they're an opportunity to lead the industry."

Mr. Thompson leaned forward, his gaze intense. "Our priority should be to preserve stability and profitability. Your plans are too drastic and may put everything we've built at risk."

Frustration simmered within Luke, but he took a steadying breath. "Respectfully, Mr. Thompson, holding onto outdated practices when the market is changing rapidly will ensure our decline. We need to be forward-thinking and embrace innovation to secure long-term success."

The tension in the room was palpable as the other board members exchanged uneasy glances. Luke's arguments had merit, but Mr. Thompson's influence was strong. It went beyond a mere business disagreement.

As the meeting concluded without a clear resolution, Luke felt a mixture of frustration and determination. He knew that persuading the board would be difficult, but his determination to advance his vision for the future of the business was undeniable.

He suggested postponing further discussions until the next board meeting. Given the thorough discussion during the meeting, he encouraged each member to take their time and ponder the shared information and insights. By giving enough time for careful analysis of the proposals, he could ensure that their decisions would benefit the organization and be well-informed. This strategic approach fostered more thoughtful discussions, leading to more effective resolutions.

As the momentous occasion of graduation approached, Sarah's heart swelled with anticipation and excitement. The years of hard work, dedication, and perseverance were finally culminating in this significant milestone. Despite the heart-wrenching loss of her parents that impacted her, she found solace and strength in her upcoming graduation from medical school, where she would soon become Dr. Sarah Bailey.

Overwhelmed by memories of her parents' unwavering support and encouragement, she prepared for this milestone with tears streaming down her face. Sarah was driven to press forward in her journey as a healthcare professional, inspired by their unwavering belief in her abilities and their loving guidance. With each determined step towards her dream, she felt the weight of their love and legacy in her heart, motivating her to make them proud and fulfill her potential.

Luke beamed with pride at Sarah's accomplishments, eager to make his way to the graduation ceremony to witness her walk across the stage and receive her well-deserved diploma. His unwavering support and presence signified a shared joy in her achievement, a testament to their bond and the shared journey that had led them to this unforgettable moment.

Sarah was grateful for Luke's support and their shared celebration of her success. Beyond being a milestone in her academic journey, graduation day symbolized the cherished bonds of friendship and the unwavering support that had guided her along the way.

Sarah and Luke sat down together, hearts full of excitement and anticipation, to discuss their intertwined plans. While planning their wedding, the conversation shifted to Sarah's upcoming residency at St. Anthony's. Luke, with a gleam of hope in his eyes, shared his vision for expanding and modernizing his family's business, weaving in his hopes for their future together. Their shared dreams and aspirations intertwined, creating a tapestry of commitment, support, and steadfast love as they navigated the promising path that lay ahead.

Sarah's smile grew wider, overcome with a wave of affection and enthusiasm, as she locked eyes with Luke. "I can't wait to see where life takes us. Our love is strong enough to conquer any challenges that come our way."

Luke reached across the table, taking Sarah's hand in his. "Together, we can achieve anything. I believe in us. Let's make our dreams a reality, starting with this wedding."

As they continued to share their aspirations, laughter and joy echoed between them, signifying the beginning of a new chapter in their lives. Their journey ahead was filled with dreams, love, and boundless possibilities.

Chapter 11

Unraveling the Past
A Mysterious Connection

Sarah's days are a whirlwind of wedding plans and the anticipation of beginning her residency under the guidance of Dr. Blake. The prospect of blending her personal and professional life fills her with a sense of adventure. However, an unexpected encounter with a stranger at the hospital shifts her world. Their brief interaction leaves her with a lingering curiosity and a newfound perspective, adding an element of mystery and unpredictability to her already bustling life.

In her office, Sarah is balancing another form of chaos. She has taken up more responsibilities in the hospital, stepping into a leadership role. Her thoughts frequently drift to the upcoming wedding. Her wedding is supposed to be a time of joy, but coordinating it with extensive work hours is demanding. Yet, every time she pictures her life entwined with Luke's, a sense of calm washes over her.

A call interrupts her day. The emergency room admits a mysterious patient who is unconscious and without identification. Sarah rushes to the ER, her curiosity piqued.

Upon arrival, she finds the patient, an older woman, hooked up to various machines, her condition critical yet stable. "What information do we have about her?" Sarah asks the attending nurse.

"Barely anything," the nurse replies. "No ID, no belongings. They found her collapsed in a park nearby."

Sarah looks at the woman, a strange sense of familiarity nagging at her mind. Ignoring the emotion, she focuses her attention on stabilizing the patient's condition. After several hours, feeling drained but with a firm resolve, she exits the ER.

By evening, Sarah and Luke meet at their favorite café, a rare moment of peace amidst the chaos. Exhausted, they still find solace in seeing each other. "How was your day?" Luke asks, taking her hand in his.

"Intense," Sarah sighs. "We admitted a patient with no ID. There's a strange feeling I have towards her... It's as if I have some familiarity with her, but I can't recall where from."

Luke squeezes her hand. "Mystery patient, huh? That's the last thing you needed."

Sarah nods, her thoughts drifting to the wedding. "Speaking of needs, we still have a wedding to organize."

"I haven't forgotten. How about we set aside a day this weekend to complete the details?" Luke suggests.

Sarah's face lights up. "I'd love that. We need to carve out time for ourselves amid all this madness."

The week passes in a whirlwind; both struggle to balance their professional duties with wedding preparations. Early mornings and late nights are common, each moment spent together a brief reprieve from their demanding schedules.

During one of those early mornings, Sarah receives an urgent hospital page just as they complete the guest lists. She kisses Luke's cheek and rushes out, promising to be back soon. The mysterious patient has regained consciousness, and Sarah needs to be there.

When Sarah arrives at the hospital, she finds the woman alert but disoriented. Her eyes hold a depth of confusion and pain, making Sarah's heart ache. "Hello," Sarah begins gently. "I'm Dr. Bailey. Could you tell me your name?"

She notices Sarah, who is standing near the window, while her eyes scan the room. She says, her voice soft, "I... I believe my name is Eleanor. Everything is so foggy."

Grasping the sensitivity of the situation, Sarah reaches out and holds Eleanor's hand. "You're safe now, Eleanor. We'll help you figure this out."

Eleanor's grip tightens. "Thank you," she says. Tears well in her eyes, uncertainty and fear palpable. Sarah stays with her, offering comfort until she drifts back to sleep.

Later that day, Luke receives a call from Sarah updating him on Eleanor's condition. Her calmness radiates through the phone. "We still have a lot to uncover about Eleanor's past. She is pivotal in a broader context."

Luke, being preoccupied with an urgent business meeting, acknowledges the gravity of the situation. "We'll get through this together. We can handle anything."

When they meet later that evening, Luke has a breakthrough in securing a vital business deal that marks his day, while Sarah makes small steps forward to uncover Eleanor's identity. They talk late into the night, their bond a testament to their enduring commitment.

As the days roll on, Sarah discovers familiar fragments about Eleanor's past. Little details—the way she speaks, subtle glances—unlock memories. One revelation stands out: a photo Eleanor had in her possessions, unnoticed before. The old, faded photo depicts a young Sarah with her family.

Sarah's heart races. Is Eleanor connected to her past? She needs answers. With mixed emotions, she sits down by Eleanor's bedside the next morning, the photo in hand. "Eleanor, I need to ask you about this," she says, showing her the picture.

Eleanor's eyes fill with tears as she looks at the photo. "I remember now," she says, her voice trembling. "I was a friend of your family, long ago. There are things you need to understand."

Sarah's mind reels, the need for answers burning brighter than ever. Is Eleanor's past a connection to her present? Can the revelation of the truth about Eleanor transform everything?

The next day, Sarah rises early and heads to the hospital, eager to talk to Eleanor and find out more details about her connection to her parents.

Sarah sits by Eleanor's bedside while she continues to recover. Eleanor's memory is still fragmented. But she has recalled details about Sarah's family, revealing long-buried secrets.

"Eleanor," Sarah says gently, "you mentioned you were close to my family. Do you think you can tell me more about what you remember?" Eleanor nods, her expression thoughtful. "Your parents… they were very private people, but they cared about making a positive impact. They had amassed significant financial wealth, which they kept hidden to protect you."

Sarah's heart races as she processes Eleanor's words. "Are you saying there is a financial trust or inheritance I wasn't aware of?" Eleanor reaches for Sarah's hand, her grip firm. "Yes, your parents set up a substantial trust fund for you, intended for use when you were ready to fulfill your dreams. They always believed in your potential to achieve greatness."

Tears well in Sarah's eyes as she absorbs the revelation. "I had no knowledge... How do I access this trust?"

Eleanor smiles, a look of relief crossing her face. "There are documents stored in a safe deposit box at the family lawyer's office. I'll give you the details, and the lawyer will explain everything to you."

With Eleanor's guidance, Sarah experiences a rush of possibilities. The newfound financial resources have the potential to impact her future, including the aspiration of establishing a specialized cardiac unit at the hospital.

Later that evening, Sarah shares the news with Luke as they sit together in their living room. "Eleanor revealed my parents left a substantial trust fund for me. We can finally make our dream of the cardiac unit a reality."

Luke's eyes light up with excitement. "That's incredible! This changes everything. Our plans can move forward much faster than we expected."

As they embrace, their hearts fill with hope and determination. The challenges they face are formidable, but they are united in their determination to create a future where their dreams and ambitions will thrive. The path ahead is uncertain, but with each other's support and newfound resources, Sarah and Luke are ready to take on whatever lies ahead.

Chapter 12

Bridging the Past and Present
Unveiling Threads

As Sarah and Luke sat in their living room, the revelations from Eleanor's recovery were still fresh in their minds. A sense of anticipation buzzed between them. The knowledge of the trust fund was a game-changer, but Eleanor had also mentioned old letters that could reveal even more about Sarah's family heritage. Curiosity and a need for closure drove them to seek these letters.

"We need to find those letters," Sarah said, determination lacing her voice. "They could have answers to questions we've never even thought to ask."

Luke nodded in complete agreement. "We should visit your parents' old house early in the morning. There might be a clue there."

The next morning, they arrived at the family estate, a place Sarah hadn't visited in years. The house stood grand and silent, a repository of memories and untapped secrets. Following Eleanor's clue about where the letters might be, they went to the attic.

As they dug through boxes of old belongings, dust particles danced in the streams of sunlight that filtered through the attic's small window. Luke opened a weathered trunk, revealing a trove of old documents and personal items. Amidst the clutter, Sarah found a bundle of letters tied together with a silk ribbon.

"I found them," she said, her voice tinged with awe. She loosened the ribbon and unfolded the initial letter, the yellowed paper making a gentle, crinkling sound.

The letters were a treasure trove of information, written by Sarah's parents to each other and to trusted friends. Through their heartfelt words, Sarah and Luke uncovered stories of resilience, hidden philanthropic efforts, and the true extent of her family's wealth and influence.

"They were incredible people," Sarah said, wiping away a tear. Their impact on many lives was significant, despite much of their work being unseen.

Luke placed an arm around her shoulders, offering silent support. "This legacy is now yours to continue, Sarah. Through our resources and these accounts, we discover motivation to enact tangible transformation."

As they absorbed the weight of these revelations, Sarah's phone buzzed with a message from the hospital. Eleanor's health had taken a sudden turn for the worse, and she was being prepped for immediate surgery. Urgency propelled them back to St. Anthony's, their minds a mix of worry and determination.

They arrived at the hospital just as Eleanor was being wheeled into surgery. Dr. Rivera, who had remained as a consultant, met them with a grave expression. "Eleanor's condition has deteriorated rapidly. We're doing everything we can, but it's critical."

Sarah nodded, her resolve hardening. "Do whatever it takes to save her, Dr. Rivera. She's important—not just to us, but to uncovering the truth about my family."

While Eleanor was in surgery, Sarah and Luke paced the waiting room, anxiety gnawing at them. Luke tried to distract Sarah with the community fundraiser plans, but her thoughts remained on Eleanor and her unanswered questions.

Hours later, Dr. Rivera emerged from the surgery room, looking exhausted but hopeful. "Eleanor made it through the surgery. She's stable but will need careful monitoring. You can see her once she's settled in the ICU."

Sarah and Luke thanked her, their minds at ease for the moment. Focus shifted to the upcoming fundraiser. Key hospital staff and local influencers mobilized to ensure the success of the fundraiser. The event was critical for gathering the support and funding needed to bring their vision for the new cardiac unit to life.

The following days were a whirlwind of preparation. Sarah worked with the hospital's PR team to complete details, while Luke coordinated logistics and reached out to potential donors. The support from the community was overwhelming, with many eager to contribute to such a meaningful cause.

The evening of the fundraiser arrived, and the hospital staff worked to transform the main atrium into a dazzling venue. Strings of lights illuminated the space, and event organizers adorned the tables with elegant centerpieces. Guests mingled, sharing stories of gratitude and support as soft music played in the background.

Sarah and Luke circulated the room, greeting attendees and sharing their vision for the cardiac unit. As they spoke, they felt the collective energy and hopefulness of the community, a testament to the impact they could achieve together.

During a brief lull, Sarah took a moment to step outside and breathe in the cool night air. She looked up at the stars, feeling a sense of peace and purpose. Luke joined her, slipping his hand into hers.

"We're really doing this," he said, his voice filled with pride. "We're making a difference."

Sarah smiled, squeezing his hand. "Yes, we are. And it's just the beginning."

Sarah felt a strong connection to her parents' legacy and the future with Luke. The evening ended on a high note, with generous donations and pledges exceeding their initial goals. The success of the fundraiser was a testament to the power of community and the enduring impact of Sarah's and Luke's commitment to their vision.

Sarah and Luke were determined to overcome challenges and secrets, with the support of friends and colleagues, to create a brighter future for the hospital and their lives together.

The days following the fundraiser were a blend of optimism and exhaustion. The success of the event had inspired the community and boosted the funds for the cardiac unit.

Sarah and Luke returned to work, but the mysteries about Eleanor and Sarah's family stayed on their minds. After a long day at the hospital, Sarah found solace in her parents' old house attic during a peaceful evening. She felt an instinctive pull towards uncovering more about her family's past, especially after the revelations from Eleanor. Luke had insisted on accompanying her, sensing the emotional weight of the task.

As they climbed up to the attic, the scent of aged wood and forgotten memories filled the air. With care, Sarah opened yet another trunk, and its ancient hinges protested with a creak. In a collection of old photo albums and childhood toys, she discovered a small box adorned with intricate decorations.

"Look at this," Sarah whispered, running her fingers over the intricate carvings. With caution, she opened the box and uncovered a diary, its weathered leather cover cracked from time.

Intrigued, Luke leaned closer. "It looks like a diary," he observed. "Could it belong to your mother?"

Nodding, Sarah could feel her heart pounding in her chest. "It is. Let's see what she wrote."

With care, she opened the diary and immersed herself in her mother's elegant handwriting. The diary revealed intimate glimpses into her parents' lives, their struggles, hopes, and unwavering love for each other and their family. While reading further, Sarah uncovered more information about the secret inheritance that someone had built to safeguard her future.

"Sarah," Luke said softly, putting a comforting hand on her shoulder. "This is incredible. Your parents went to such lengths to protect and provide for you."

Sarah wiped away a tear, her emotions a whirlwind. "They were amazing people. I always knew they were special, but this... it means so much more knowing the sacrifices they made."

While examining the diary further, they stumbled upon entries alluding to a hereditary illness that had plagued Sarah's great-grandmother. The symptoms described in the diary bore a striking resemblance to Eleanor's condition.

"This could be the key to understanding Eleanor's illness," Sarah said, her voice tinged with urgency. "We need to share this with her medical team immediately."

Luke agreed to the plan, so they wasted no time photocopying the relevant pages before making their way back to the hospital. Eleanor's condition had been stable but precarious, and these new insights could be crucial in managing her treatment.

At the hospital, Dr. Rivera and the medical team pored over the diary entries. "This information is invaluable," Dr. Rivera said, looking up from the pages. "It gives us a clearer picture of the genetic factors at play. We can adjust Eleanor's treatment accordingly."

Relieved, Sarah and Luke found a potential solution to save Eleanor and discussed their next actions.

Luke had scheduled a meeting with his previous mentor, Mr. Carter, who had offered to help him with his business endeavors. Luke and Mr. Carter had a meeting the next day in a high-rise office that overlooked the city. Luke received a warm welcome from Mr. Carter, a skilled businessman with a sharp mind and insightful perspective.

"It's been too long, Luke," Mr. Carter began, a hint of nostalgia in his voice. "I hear you've taken some bold steps with the family business."

Luke explained his vision for the company's future, his ideas for sustainability, and his struggles with the board, especially Mr. Thompson's resistance.

Mr. Carter's face lit up with a radiant smile, his eyes sparkling with excitement, as he nodded, engrossed in the engaging conversation. "Luke, you're heading in the right direction. Today's market demands both innovation and sustainability. In order to gain the board's support, you must employ tactical methods. Focus on presenting undeniable data and case studies that highlight the benefits without threatening the status quo."

"I... I really value your advice," Luke stammered, his voice trembling, betraying his underlying anxiety.

"Certain board members cling to their own viewpoints, causing an atmosphere of unease and uncertainty to permeate the room," he stated.

"Stick to your convictions," Mr. Carter encouraged. "Show them the long-term gains and how it aligns with our fundamental business principles. And remember, bringing allies to your side will strengthen your position." With renewed confidence, Luke left the meeting, ready to tackle the board with a bolstered strategy and Mr. Carter's invaluable insights. Meanwhile, back at the hospital, Sarah found herself more connected than ever to her family's legacy and the responsibilities it entailed.

As Sarah and Luke reconvened that evening, they couldn't help but marvel at the twists and turns life had thrown their way. Together, they had navigated immense challenges and uncovered profound secrets. With each other's support, they felt prepared to face whatever the future held, bound by love and a shared determination to honor the legacies passed down to them.

As Sarah and Luke sat in their living room, the weight of recent revelations still lingering between them, a sense of anxious anticipation hung in the air. The trust fund and old letters had unraveled new mysteries about Sarah's family, but they felt more needed to be uncovered.

Now, with Eleanor's condition and the upcoming wedding, their minds whirled with thoughts about the future.

"We need to be prepared for whatever comes next," Luke said, breaking the silence, his eyes fixed on Sarah. "There's so much happening, and we need to make sure we stay grounded."

"I know," Sarah said, her voice tinged doggedly. "The wedding is so close, and with Eleanor's health improving, we're on the brink of something huge."

Just as they were about to delve deeper into their conversation, Sarah's phone buzzed with an incoming call from Dr. Rivera. She answered, her breath held in anticipation.

"Sarah, I have news," Dr. Rivera said, a hint of excitement in her voice. "Eleanor has regained more of her memories. She asked to see you and Luke immediately."

"We'll be right there, Dr. Rivera," Sarah said, her heart pounding. She shared the news with Luke. Gathering their things, they headed toward the hospital with a mixture of hope and apprehension.

Upon arriving, they found Eleanor sitting up in bed, looking more alert and aware than ever before. She managed a wan smile as they entered the room.

"Sarah, Luke, thank you for coming," Eleanor said softly, her voice still shaky. "I have remembered something important—something that changes everything."

Sarah sat beside her, taking Eleanor's hand in hers. "What is it, Eleanor? What did you remember?"

Eleanor took a deep breath, steadying herself. "My memory of my family has improved. I am not just a friend to your family, Sarah. I am your mother's half-sister."

"My mother's half-sister? How?" Sarah's voice trembled with shock and curiosity.

"Your grandmother had an affair before marrying your grandfather," Eleanor explained, her eyes glistening with emotion. "I resulted from that affair. They kept it secret to protect the family. After your grandfather passed away, your parents supported my mother and me, albeit discreetly."

Luke squeezed Sarah's shoulder, offering silent support. This revelation was monumental, adding another layer to Sarah's understanding of her family's complex history.

"So your genetic illness," Sarah murmured, connecting the dots. "That explains it. We share the same bloodline."

"Yes," Eleanor said. "I sensed something was amiss upon first seeing you. Now, everything makes sense."

The emotional weight of the revelation hung in the air, a mix of sorrow and newfound connection. Sarah leaned over and hugged Eleanor, tears streaming down her face.

"We're family," Sarah whispered, her heart heavy with both relief and sorrow.

As they absorbed the significance of Eleanor's revelation, a hospital administrator entered, carrying a letter. "Ms. Phillips, Mr. Thompson has requested a meeting to discuss a potential benefactor for the cardiac unit. He said it's urgent."

Sarah and Luke exchanged puzzled glances but agreed to the meeting. Moments later, they found themselves in a conference room with Mr. Thompson and a mysterious man in a tailored suit.

"Please meet Mr. Harrison Blackwood," Mr. Thompson introduced, his tone formal. "Mr. Blackwood is prepared to offer substantial support for our cardiac unit, under certain conditions."

Harrison Blackwood nodded, his aura exuding confidence. "Thank you for meeting with me on such short notice. I'm deeply invested in advancing cardiac care. My support comes with specific stipulations, designed to ensure the excellence and sustainability of the unit."

Sarah felt a mix of excitement and wariness. "We appreciate your offer, Mr. Blackwood. Could you elaborate on these conditions?"

Harrison smiled, his gaze unwavering. "Certainly. My conditions primarily revolve around adopting state-of-the-art technologies, ensuring transparent governance, and establishing an annual review committee to maintain the highest standards."

Luke nodded. "These sound like reasonable expectations. However, we need to ensure these conditions align with our existing protocols and that they truly benefit patient care."

"Absolutely," Harrison agreed. "I assure you, my interest lies solely in advancing healthcare. I'm more than willing to collaborate on necessary adjustments to suit the hospital's needs."

After a lengthy discussion, Harrison's intentions aligned with the hospital's goals. The agreement promised to bring significant advancements and resources to the cardiac unit, marking a turning point in their mission.

As they wrapped up the meeting, Sarah and Luke couldn't help but feel a renewed sense of hope and determination. The mysterious benefactor's support and Eleanor's revelations had set the stage for a brighter future.

Sarah and Luke left the meeting with Harrison Blackwood, feeling a mix of reassurance and trepidation. The promise of substantial support for the cardiac unit was a beacon of hope, but they knew that more challenges lay ahead.

Sarah and Luke embraced upcoming challenges and opportunities as they approached their wedding day, confident in their ability to create lasting change for their community and their lives together.

Chapter 13

The Weight of Destinies

Eleanor's revelation about their shared family history had brought them closer, and as they navigated the hospital corridors, the complexities of intertwined destinies weighed on their minds.

"Eleanor really turned our world upside down, didn't she?" Luke mused, breaking the contemplative silence between them.

Sarah nodded, her expression thoughtful. "I didn't expect to find out I had more family, especially not under these circumstances. But I'm grateful we discovered the truth. We need to focus on her recovery now while we push forward with the cardiac unit."

They headed to Eleanor's room, intending to update her on the meeting with Harrison Blackwood. However, the moment they arrived, they realized something was amiss. The medical team gathered around Eleanor's bed, their faces showing concern.

"What's happening?" Sarah asked, her stomach tightening with dread.

Dr. Rivera turned to them, her expression grave. "Eleanor's condition has suddenly deteriorated. We're running more tests to determine the cause, but it's not looking good. Something beyond hereditary illness is in play here."

Sarah felt a wave of helplessness wash over her. "How can we be of help?"

"Right now, we need to wait for the test results," Dr. Rivera replied. "It would also help if we had more detailed records of your family's medical history. There may be undiscovered clues there."

Luke squeezed Sarah's hand. "We'll start looking into it right away. Hang in there, Eleanor."

Sarah's mind is racing through possibilities as they leave Eleanor's room. "There is a possibility the documents we're looking for are still at my parents' house. We should try searching again."

Luke nodded. "We'll find whatever we can. Let's go now."

They hurried back to the family estate, their resolve unshaken by the urgency of the situation. In the attic, they sifted through every box, drawer, and trunk, leaving no stone unturned. Hours passed, and just as exhaustion threatened to overtake them, Sarah stumbled upon an old, locked chest they hadn't noticed before.

"Luke, look at this," she said, her voice filled with hope. "Could this hold the answers we need?"

Luke examined the chest, finding an intricate keyhole. "We need to find the key. Check around the old trunks and shelves; it has to be here somewhere."

After a frantic search, they finally found a small, ornate key hidden in a desk drawer. Sarah inserted it into the lock, holding her breath as she turned it. The chest opened with a soft creak, revealing a trove of organized files and letters.

"This has to be it," Sarah said, her heart pounding. "We should bring these to the hospital and review them with Dr. Rivera."

They packed the documents and returned to St. Anthony's, hope flickering in their eyes. Dr. Rivera joined them in Eleanor's room, and together, they pored over the newfound records. Among the papers, they discovered detailed medical histories that showed a rare genetic disorder affecting multiple generations of Sarah's family.

"This could be the breakthrough we needed," Dr. Rivera said, her voice tinged with optimism. "With this information, we can adjust Eleanor's treatment plan and stabilize her condition."

Sarah felt a surge of relief and gratitude. "Thank you, Dr. Rivera. Eleanor means a lot to us."

Eleanor received the new treatment while Sarah and Luke allowed themselves a moment of respite.

But their relief was short-lived as Sarah's phone alarm reminded her of the upcoming wedding date and the unfinished tasks.

"We can't let the wedding fall apart now," Luke said, determination in his voice. "What should be our next focus?"

Sarah glanced at their to-do list, a sense of panic rising. "We need to complete the guest list, confirm our venue, and handle a dozen other details. It's overwhelming, but we can manage it. We have to."

Just as they began tackling the wedding arrangements, an unforeseen event disrupted their plans. A massive storm system moved into the area, causing widespread damage and power outages. The venue they had secured for their wedding became unusable for the foreseeable future because of the impact of a massive storm system that moved into the area.

"This can't be happening," Sarah said, staring at the news report in disbelief. "We've come so far. Now, what do we do?"

Luke put an arm around her, offering solace. "Sarah, we'll discover an alternative solution. We'll reach out to everyone we know to see if there's a backup venue available. We can't let this stop us."

Despite the setback, Sarah and Luke began making calls and exploring alternative arrangements. Friends, family, and the community rallied around them, offering help and support. They received a promising lead on a picturesque outdoor location that the storm had spared.

"It's not what we originally planned, but it could be perfect," Sarah said, a flicker of hope returning to her eyes. "Let's make sure everything works out."

The new venue was breathtaking. The backdrop for their wedding was serene and magical.

With renewed determination, they completed the details, ensuring that their special day would proceed despite the hurdles they had faced.

Walking hand-in-hand through the venue, surrounded by the beauty of nature, Sarah and Luke felt a deep sense of gratitude and unity. They had faced countless challenges together, and their love and commitment had only strengthened through each trial.

"No matter what happens, we'll always have each other," Luke said, pulling Sarah close. "This wedding will be perfect because it's about us and our journey together."

"I couldn't agree more," Sarah said, a contented smile spreading across her face. "Together, we can handle anything."

With the new venue secured and their wedding plans back on track, Sarah and Luke returned to their responsibilities at St. Anthony's and the family business. Despite the stress of wedding preparations, they found solace in each other's presence, knowing that their love could overcome any obstacle.

Eleanor's condition, however, remained a pressing concern, and they visited her regularly, hoping for more improvements in her health and memory.

During one such visit, they found Eleanor sitting up in bed, a renewed strength clear in her eyes. She greeted them with a warm smile, and as they settled into chairs beside her bed, she said in a clear, steady voice.

"Sarah, Luke, I have remembered something important." Her tone was serious. "There is another secret that your family kept hidden. It concerns the new venue for your wedding."

Sarah and Luke exchanged puzzled glances. "The new venue? What about it?" Sarah asked, leaning forward with curiosity.

Eleanor nodded, her expression thoughtful. "That location has a significant history tied to your family. It belonged to your great-grandparents years ago. The place held both immense joy and sorrow for them."

Intrigued, Sarah urged Eleanor to continue. "What happened there? Could you tell me why it's so important?"

"Your great-grandparents, William and Florence, used that venue for many family gatherings and celebrations," Eleanor explained. "It was a symbol of their love and unity. However, it was also where a tragic event occurred."

Luke placed a comforting hand on Sarah's shoulder as she absorbed Eleanor's words. "What kind of tragedy?" Sarah asked.

Eleanor took a deep breath, her eyes reflecting the weight of the story. "During one of their anniversaries, a fire broke out, claiming the lives of several family members. The loss was devastating, and the family abandoned the property for years. When they finally restored it, lingering memories of both joy and sorrow remained with them."

Sarah felt a shiver run down her spine. "I did not know. This place holds so much history."

"Yes," her gentle voice agreed. "But it also holds the strength and resilience of your family. They rebuilt their lives after the tragedy, just as you and Luke have faced and overcome many challenges together."

Luke squeezed Sarah's hand, offering silent support. "We should honor their memory during our wedding," he said. "It could be a way to acknowledge our family's past while looking forward to our future."

Sarah nodded, feeling a sense of purpose. "You're right, Luke. We'll incorporate something meaningful into the ceremony. Thank you, Eleanor, for sharing this with us."

As they left Eleanor's room, Sarah and Luke felt a renewed connection to their family heritage. They spent the next few days making plans to honor their ancestors during the wedding, ensuring that they would remember and cherish their legacy.

On the day of the wedding, the wedding planner transformed the new venue into a breathtaking setting. Strings of lights adorned the trees, and delicate floral arrangements lined the pathway. Guests arrived, their faces filled with anticipation and joy. Sarah and Luke had planned a small tribute to their great-grandparents with a moment of silence and a brief story about the history of the venue.

As the ceremony began, Sarah walked down the aisle, her heart pounding with a mix of excitement and emotion. Luke waited at the altar, his eyes brimming with love as he watched his bride approach. When they finally stood together, hand in hand, the officiant spoke.

"Today, we gather not only to celebrate Sarah and Luke's union but also to honor the legacy of their families," the officiant said. "This venue holds a significant history, a testament to the strength and resilience of those who came before them."

The tribute to William and Florence brought tears to many eyes, and Sarah felt a deep sense of connection to her heritage. As they exchanged vows, she felt her ancestors, their love and support guiding her.

"I vow to stand by you through every challenge and triumph," her voice steady despite the tears. "To honor our past and build a bright future together."

Luke smiled, his own emotions reflected in his eyes. "I vow to love you unconditionally, to support and cherish you. Together, we will create a legacy of our own, rooted in the strength of our families."

As they sealed their vows with a kiss, the guests erupted in applause, their cheers echoing through the venue. Laughter, dancing, and heartfelt toasts filled the reception that followed. Sarah and Luke moved through the crowd, feeling the warmth and support of their loved ones.

Later that evening, as the celebration continued under the stars, Sarah and Luke took a moment to themselves, standing where William and Florence once stood. They felt a sense of closure and peace, knowing that they were part of a larger story, one that spanned generations.

"We did it," Luke said softly, pulling Sarah close. "We've honored our past and embraced our future."

Sarah nodded, her heart full. "And we'll continue to face whatever comes our way together."

Hand in hand, they looked out at the surrounding celebration, ready to embark on the next chapter of their lives, guided by love, resilience, and the unbreakable bond of family.

Chapter 14

Reflections and Resilience

As the wedding celebrations continued under the soft glow of string lights, Sarah and Luke stepped away from the crowd, seeking a quiet moment in the venue's old garden. The air carried the scent of fresh blooms and the distant hum of laughter and music.

"It's surreal, isn't it?" Sarah murmured, resting her head on Luke's shoulder. "Everything we've learned about our families, and now this beautiful day."

Luke nodded, his arm wrapped around her. "And it's just the beginning. The start of our own story, built on the legacy of those who came before us."

They wandered through the garden, their steps slow and deliberate. As they reached a secluded corner, Sarah noticed something partially hidden under an ancient oak tree–a small, weathered box, its wood aged and worn. Intrigued, she pointed it out to Luke.

"Look at that," she whispered, her curiosity piqued. "Do you think it could be another piece of the puzzle?"

Luke knelt beside the box, carefully lifting it from its resting place. "Only one way to find out," he replied, opening the box with a gentle tug. Inside, they discovered an old journal, its leather cover embossed with the initials W and F.

"William and Florence," Sarah whispered, her heart racing. "This must have been theirs."

They settled onto a nearby bench, eager to delve into the journal's contents. As Sarah read, William and Florence's lives unfolded before them, each page revealing their joys, sorrows, and the challenges they faced together.

"They loved this place," Sarah said, her voice filled with wonder. "It was their sanctuary, just as it's become ours."

Luke leaned closer, pointing to a particular entry. "Look at this–it's about the fire Eleanor mentioned. They tried to rebuild, but the loss was too great. Yet, despite everything, they never lost hope."

The journal's pages vividly portrayed resilience and love, qualities that were clearly passed down through the generations. As they read on, Sarah and Luke came across a mention of a hidden heirloom, something William and Florence had deemed essential to their family's legacy.

"An heirloom?" Luke pondered. "Do you think it could still be here somewhere?"

"It's possible," Sarah replied, her determination rekindled. "We should try to find it. It could hold important keys to understanding our past even further."

Just as they were making plans to search, Sarah's phone buzzed with a call from the hospital. Eleanor had made a miraculous recovery and was asking to see them urgently. Sharing a look of astonishment and relief, they rushed back to St. Anthony's.

In Eleanor's room, they found her sitting up, her eyes sparkling with vitality. "Sarah, Luke," she says warmly, "I've remembered everything now, and there's something vital I need to tell you both."

Sarah took Eleanor's hand, her heart soaring with hope. "What is it, Eleanor? What do you remember?"

Eleanor took a deep breath, her expression growing serious. "The hidden heirloom your great-grandparents mentioned in the journal–it's a key to a family treasure hidden in this venue. It's meant to secure your future and help you carry on their legacy."

Luke's eyes widened in surprise. "A treasure? Where is it hidden?"

"William and Florence left clues in their belongings. It won't be easy to find, but with determination, I'm certain you can uncover it," Eleanor replied, her voice steady. "This treasure is more than just wealth; it's a testament to your family's strength and perseverance."

Sarah and Luke exchanged determined glances. "We need to find it, Luke. For our future and for our family."

"Absolutely," Luke agreed. "We'll start searching as soon as we can."

As they left Eleanor's room, their minds raced with possibilities. Just as they thought they were understanding their family's story, new layers of history and legacy emerged, challenging them to dig deeper and uncover the full truth.

Amid the quest for the heirloom, another storm was brewing — this time at Luke's business. He had received word of a potentially hostile takeover attempt by a rival company seeking to undermine his leadership and seize control of the family's hard-earned empire.

"I can't believe this is happening now," Luke muttered as he and Sarah drove back home. "We need to protect the business and our family's legacy."

Sarah reached over, offering a reassuring squeeze of his hand. "We'll face this together, Luke. Just like everything else. Our family has weathered storms before, and we will, too."

Determined to safeguard their future, Sarah and Luke prepared to navigate the complex world of corporate intrigue and protect what mattered most to them. With the strength they drew from each other and the wisdom of their ancestors, they felt ready to face whatever challenges awaited them.

Sarah and Luke arrived back at the old family estate, the urgency and anticipation palpable in the air. The discovery of the heirloom mentioned by Eleanor had filled them with a renewed sense of purpose. They hoped that finding this hidden treasure would not only secure their future but also deepen their connection to their roots.

"We need to start where we left off, near the old oak tree in the garden," Luke said, determination etched on his face. They had already found William and Florence's journal, which had given them clues about the heirloom's significance. Now, they needed to uncover its exact location.

As they approached the oak tree, Sarah felt a familiar rush of excitement mixed with trepidation. With every step, she sensed the weight of her ancestors watching over them, guiding their path. "Let's look for any hidden markings or unusual features around the tree," she suggested.

They meticulously began searching the area around the old oak, examining the tree's trunk and its base. Luke ran his hands over the rough bark, hoping to feel any irregularities. Minutes turned into hours, and just as Sarah was about to voice her frustration, Luke's fingers brushed against a small, engraved symbol partly hidden by the moss.

"Sarah, come look at this!" Luke called out, excitement tinging his voice. She hurried over, her heart racing as she saw the symbol—a combination of their family crest and a key motif.

"This must be it," Sarah said, tracing the engravings with reverence. "It looks like a lock of some sort."

Luke pulled out a small, worn key they had found in the trunk with the journal. It seemed a perfect fit for the engraving. With fingers trembling slightly, he inserted the key and turned it. A section of the tree's base shifted, revealing a concealed compartment.

Inside, they found a beautifully ornate box. The craftsmanship was exquisite, with intricate designs and precious gems inlaid on its surface. Sarah gently lifted the box out, her breath hitching in anticipation. "This is it, Luke. This is what our ancestors wanted us to find."

They opened the box together, revealing a trove of gold coins, old family documents, and a meticulously bound book. The book's title, still legible after all these years, read: "The Legacy of Innovation: Strategies for Business Resilience and Growth."

"This book... it's a business strategy manual," Luke gasped, thumbing through the pages. "It's filled with century-old principles and methods. Look at this, Sarah! These ideas are incredibly forward-thinking, still relevant today."

Sarah's eyes widened as she scanned the pages. "This could revolutionize our approach, Luke. It's exactly what we need to combat the takeover and protect the family business."

They spent the next few hours poring over the contents of the book, their excitement growing with each discovery. The manual contained innovative ideas on leadership, sustainability, and market expansion—strategies that could give them a significant edge.

As evening fell, they knew they couldn't waste any time implementing these newfound strategies. Luke prepared to confront the CEO of the rival company the next day, armed with the innovative ideas from the heirloom discovery.

The following morning, Luke walked into the rival company's headquarters, his demeanor calm and confident. He had scheduled a meeting with Mr. Andrews, the CEO intent on the hostile takeover, to offer a counter-proposal.

"Thank you for meeting with me, Mr. Andrews," Luke began, extending a hand. "I believe we can find a solution that benefits both our companies."

Mr. Andrews, a shrewd businessman with a keen eye for opportunities, eyed Luke curiously. "I'm listening," he said, steepling his fingers.

Luke laid out his plan, integrating the innovative strategies from the book. His proposal included a collaborative approach to market expansion and sustainability initiatives that would benefit both companies while preserving his family's legacy.

"These strategies are not just about survival, Mr. Andrews," Luke explained. "They're about thriving in an evolving market. We can achieve more together than in opposition."

Mr. Andrews leaned back, considering the proposal. "You've presented a compelling case, Mr. Hamilton. These ideas are indeed innovative. I'll need to confer with my board, but I see potential in this collaboration."

Relief washed over Luke as Mr. Andrews agreed to delay the takeover attempt and consider the partnership. He left the meeting feeling triumphant, knowing that the risk had paid off.

Back at the hospital, Sarah received notification of Luke's success. They reunited in Eleanor's room, sharing the news with her and feeling the collective weight of their responsibilities lifting slightly.

"We did it, Eleanor," Sarah said, her voice filled with gratitude. "We've secured the business and uncovered a treasure that ensures our future. Thank you for guiding us to this moment."

Eleanor smiled, her eyes twinkling with pride. "Your family's legacy is in excellent hands. Continue to honor it, and you'll achieve great things."

As Sarah and Luke embraced, they felt more connected than ever—to each other, to their past, and to the bright future that lay ahead. With resilience, love, and newfound wisdom, they were ready to face whatever came next, confident in their ability to build a legacy that would endure for generations.

Chapter 15

Bonds of Healing and Unity

Sarah and Luke stood hand in hand in Eleanor's room, basking in their collective success. They had secured the future of the family business, discovered an invaluable heirloom, and strengthened their bond with each other. However, as the sun set, casting a golden hue over St. Anthony's Hospital, an uneasy tension permeated the air.

Just as they were about to leave, the hospital intercom blared with an urgent announcement.

"Attention all medical staff: we have identified a new and rapidly spreading illness. All available personnel, please report to the emergency room immediately."

Sarah and Luke exchanged concerned glances. "We need to see what's happening," Sarah said, her voice steady despite the ominous news. "Let's go."

They rushed to the emergency room, where a flurry of activity greeted them. Patients filled the beds and stretchers, each showing symptoms of a mysterious illness. Doctors and nurses moved with frantic precision, managing the influx.

Dr. Rivera noticed Sarah and Luke entering and approached them. "Thank goodness you're here," she said, her voice strained. "We've seen nothing like this before. The symptoms are acute respiratory distress, high fever, and severe fatigue."

Sarah felt a surge of determination. "We need to contain this and identify the source. Do we have any leads on patient zero?"

Dr. Rivera shook her head. "Not yet. But we have a new specialist joining us. Dr. Adrian Blackwood. He's renowned for his work in infectious diseases and has agreed to assist us."

A man, tall and mysterious, arrived. His sharp features and intense gaze commanded attention. "Dr. Blackwood," he introduced himself, extending a hand. "I understand this is an urgent situation. Let's get to work."

Sarah and Luke felt a flicker of hope. "We're grateful for your help, Dr. Blackwood," Sarah said, shaking his hand. "Let's coordinate our efforts and find a solution."

The next few hours were a blur of examinations, tests, and consultations. Dr. Blackwood's expertise became apparent as he directed the team with confidence and precision. Despite the chaos, a sense of camaraderie formed among the staff.

Later, as they gathered in a conference room to review their findings, Luke noticed a familiar face among the crowd. His expression tightened as he recognized his estranged sibling, Rachel, standing near the entrance. "Rachel?" he called out, surprise and tension clear in his voice. "What are you doing here?"

Rachel approached with caution, her eyes reflecting a mix of emotions. "I came to help," she admitted. "I've been working in public health and heard about the crisis. It's hard to stay away."

Luke's initial shock gave way to a sense of opportunity. If you're here to help, let's move forward and focus on the task.

Dr. Blackwood observed the exchange with interest. "If Rachel has experience in public health, her insights could be invaluable," he noted. "We should welcome her expertise."

Sarah, sensing the importance of unity, nodded in agreement. "Absolutely. Rachel, we could use all the help we can get."

With Rachel's inclusion, the team felt more cohesive. They divided tasks, with Rachel focusing on tracing patient zero while Dr. Blackwood led the diagnostic efforts. Sarah and Luke orchestrated the overall coordination, ensuring seamless communication among the staff.

By dawn, a breakthrough emerged. Rachel had identified a potential source of the illness—an infected shipment of medical supplies. "We need to isolate and recall those supplies immediately," she advised. "And we should also notify other hospitals that may have received the same shipment."

Dr. Blackwood concurred, planning containment and treatment based on the findings. "Let's act quickly," he urged. "We can mitigate the spread if we move now."

The following hours were tense but productive. The team implemented the containment protocols, and the hospital stabilized. Patients received targeted treatments, showing gradual signs of improvement.

As calm returned to the hospital, Sarah and Luke stood with Rachel, reflecting on the day's events. "We did it," Sarah said, her voice filled with gratitude. "This crisis could have been catastrophic, but we contained it."

Luke turned to Rachel, a hint of reconciliation in his eyes. "Thank you for helping us. It means a lot."

Rachel smiled, the tension between them easing. "I'm glad I could contribute. This is a chance for us to rebuild our relationship."

With the immediate crisis averted, they felt a renewed sense of purpose. But as they returned to Eleanor's room, a new discovery awaited them—ancient family letters hidden among her possessions.

Sarah opened one letter, revealing a correspondence that hinted at a hidden philanthropic foundation created by their ancestors. "Luke, look at this," she said, her excitement growing. "Our family established a foundation to support the community. It is essential to uncover more and increase its impact."

As the dawn of a new day broke, Sarah and Luke felt invigorated by the knowledge of their ancestors' legacy. With renewed determination, they prepared to explore the hidden foundation, ready to bring its mission to life and further their positive impact on the community.

Luke made plans to meet Rachel in the boardroom at the family business that morning. As they stood in the boardroom, their shared history was palpable but now threaded together. The hospital crisis had formed a fragile truce between them and now was the time to confront the unresolved issues that had persisted for too long.

"Rachel," Luke began, his voice steady but filled with emotion, "I've been thinking a lot about our past and the misunderstandings that pulled us apart. It's time we faced those issues head-on and rebuilt our partnership for the sake of our family and the business."

Rachel met his gaze, her expression a mix of resolve and vulnerability. "I agree, Luke. We can't change the past, but we can shape the future. Let's put everything on the table and move forward together."

They spent hours in deep conversation, unpacking years of tension and miscommunication. Luke acknowledged his shortcomings, while Rachel shared her frustrations and desires for a more collaborative approach. Through honesty and mutual respect, a new understanding emerged.

"I never wanted to vie with you, Rachel," Luke said earnestly. "I only wanted what was best for our family and the business." Now, I realize our potential is greater through collaboration.

Rachel nodded, her eyes shimmering with tears of relief. "I've always admired your vision and dedication. Let's combine our strengths and make this business something our parents will be proud of."

With a renewed sense of unity, they solidified plans to address key business challenges and explore new opportunities. Rachel accepted Luke's offer to join the company's leadership, bringing her expertise and fresh perspectives to the table. It marked the start of a partnership that was stronger and more resilient, becoming a turning point.

At the hospital, Sarah stood before a gathering of staff and community members, introducing their philanthropic foundation. The room buzzed with excitement and anticipation as she unveiled the foundation's mission to support healthcare, education, and innovation in their community and beyond.

"This foundation is not just a testament to our family's legacy," Sarah said, her voice filled with passion. "It's a commitment to making a lasting impact, to leaving the world better than we found it. Today, we take our first steps toward partnering with international organizations to amplify our efforts and reach more people in need."

The audience applauded and discussed the possibilities that lay ahead in response to the announcement. As the meeting concluded, a young journalist approached Sarah and Luke, her eyes alight with curiosity and determination.

"Hi, I'm Emily Thompson," she introduced herself, extending a hand. "I've been following your journey and would love to document your story. It has the power to inspire change and uncover untold narratives."

Luke shook her hand, intrigued by her enthusiasm. "Nice to meet you, Emily. We're happy to share our experiences. What do you have in mind?"

Emily smiled, her passion clear. "I would like to capture the challenges, triumphs, and personal stories behind your efforts. Let's delve into the impact of the foundation, the progress at the hospital, and the dynamics of your family business. Your journey can spark a ripple effect of positive change."

Sarah and Luke exchanged approving glances. "We're in," Sarah said, her voice steady with conviction. "Let's work together and bring these stories to light."

Over the next few weeks, Emily immersed herself in their world, documenting every step of their journey. She interviewed staff, patients, and community members, uncovering heartfelt testimonials and transformative moments. Her articles, filled with vivid storytelling and impactful visuals, resonated with readers, drawing attention and support from far and wide.

Through Emily's work, the foundation gained visibility, leading to new partnerships with international organizations. Projects that once seemed like distant dreams now materialized, bringing healthcare, education, and innovation to underserved communities across the globe.

As Sarah and Luke watched the positive effects of their efforts ripple outward, they felt a profound sense of fulfillment and responsibility. They had embraced their family's legacy and forged a path forward, united by love and a shared vision for a better world.

One evening, as they stood in the garden of their family estate, Sarah turned to Luke, her eyes reflecting the stars above. "We've come so far. There is still much left to do."

Luke smiled, wrapping an arm around her. "And we'll do it together. With each new challenge, we'll grow stronger and more united. Our journey is just beginning, and the possibilities are endless."

Hand in hand, they looked out at the world they were helping to shape, ready to face whatever came next with resilience, passion, and an unwavering bond.

Chapter 16

Balancing the Scales

The stars shimmered above the family estate. Sarah and Luke held each other, feeling a strong connection. Sarah's phone buzzed, shattering the tranquility. Dr. Rivera's name flashed on the screen, causing her stomach to tighten as she answered, uncertain about the reason for her call. "Hello, Dr. Rivera. Is everything okay?"

"Sarah, come to the hospital." Dr. Rivera's urgent voice came through. "Eleanor's condition has worsened."

Fear gripped Sarah's heart as she understood the implications. She turned to Luke, her eyes filled with dread. "Eleanor is critical. We need to go now." Without wasting a moment, they rushed to the car and sped toward St. Anthony's, the tranquility of the night replaced by a surge of anxiety. The thought of losing Eleanor, their newfound family connection, was unbearable.

As they entered the hospital, they spotted Dr. Rivera, whose somber expression conveyed the seriousness of the situation. "Eleanor's situation is critical. It appears her immune system is collapsing, and we need to stabilize her."

Sarah felt the weight of the imminent decisions pressing down on her. "What are our options, Dr. Rivera?"

Luke took a step forward, the sound of his firm footsteps echoing through the room. The air was heavy with anticipation as he spoke, his voice filled with genuine concern. "Is there anything specific we can do to offer our support? We will take any necessary measures. She holds a vital place within our family, and the mere thought of her absence is unfathomable."

Dr. Rivera's tone carried a sense of worry as she spoke. "To save her life. Eleanor's medical team is considering an innovative treatment that carries its own unique risk. I can't emphasize enough the urgency of having a reliable support system. Pray for her healing and the success of our medical team in providing her with the care she needs."

As the medical team prepared for Eleanor's treatment the next morning, Sarah and Luke struggled with conflicting responsibilities. The family business required Luke's attention, especially with the recent partnership and the growing demands. The hospital needed Sarah for Eleanor and the crisis management.

Sarah's determined tone conveyed a simple message to Luke, urging him to return to the office and attend to the business tasks. "I have decided that I will not leave and will stay here alongside Eleanor."

Luke hesitated, torn between his duties. "Are you sure, Sarah? I don't want to leave you alone here."

Sarah nodded, her eyes reflecting strength. "Yes, I'm sure. We need to divide and conquer. Eleanor needs me, and the business needs you."

With a heavy heart, Luke agreed, understanding the need for their decision. He kissed Sarah's forehead, his voice tender yet firm. "Call me if anything changes. I'll be back as soon as I can."

As Luke walked away, Sarah concentrated all her attention on Eleanor. She held her aunt's hand, whispering words of encouragement, hoping her presence would provide some comfort. The hours passed in a blur as the medical team worked nonstop, their collective efforts fueled by a desire to save Eleanor's life.

During a brief lull, Sarah reflected on the dual responsibilities she and Luke were shouldering. The balance between family and business was delicate and often brutal. But she knew their strength lay in their unity and determination to support each other, no matter the cost.

Dr. Blackwood walked up to Sarah, looking exhausted yet hopeful. "The treatment is showing initial positive signs. There's hope despite the challenges," he said. Sarah felt relieved but still tense. "Thank you, Dr. Blackwood. We're grateful for all your efforts."

Sarah continued to keep vigil by Eleanor's bedside, her thoughts oscillating between worry and hope. She was determined not to lose her aunt, the link to her family's past and the bearer of truths she'd only just uncovered.

Luke faced fresh challenges at the office. With his impressive ability to navigate through many meetings and conference calls, he rallied the team to stay focused on their new initiatives and keep them on track. Despite their separation, he found comfort in knowing that Sarah's presence was always with him, giving him the strength and inspiration he needed.

In a video call with Rachel, Luke outlined the immediate steps they needed to take to move forward with the next phase of expansion. "We can't afford to lose momentum now. Every decision we make has to be strategic and aligned with our vision."

Rachel nodded, her support palpable through the screen. "We're in this together, Luke. Let's make every move count."

As the first rays of the sun emerged, they brought with them a sense of relief that lifted the weight of the night. When Sarah and the entire team at St. Anthony's saw that Eleanor's condition had stabilized, it filled them with relief and gave them hope for her recovery.

Luke's face displayed traces of weariness as he returned to the hospital, but his eyes sparkled with excitement. Without wasting a moment, he walked towards Sarah and wrapped his arms around her, giving her a warm embrace. "How is she?" He asked.

"She's improving," Sarah said, her voice choked with tears and her eyes glistening. "Although the situation remains critical, my hope has never been stronger."

Sarah and Luke's determination helps them overcome adversity and find hope at the tunnel's end.

Together, they could sense the immense burden of the challenges they had overcome and the indomitable power they had derived from their mutual support.

"We've come so far," Luke said, his voice filled with pride as he held Sarah close. "Together, we've weathered countless storms and conquered many obstacles. We just need to keep going forward."

With a nod, Sarah's heart filled with a mixture of love and determination, causing it to swell. "No matter what happens, we'll always face it together." She said.

As they walked back to join Eleanor and the medical team, Sarah and Luke felt a renewed sense of purpose and unity. Their journey was far from over, but they were ready to face whatever came next, confident in their bond and driven by the legacy they were building together.

Chapter 17

Charting a New Course - A Vision for Family Business Transformation

Luke and Rachel have dedicated themselves to repairing their strained relationship as they stand side by side, united, charging the atmosphere in the boardroom with anticipation. Prepared to present an innovative proposal aiming to revolutionize their family business.

With Rachel's support, Luke faces the expectant board members who have gathered to hear about this transformative vision.

Rachel takes the lead, addressing the room, her gaze sweeping over the familiar faces with a mixture of confidence and excitement. "I would like to express my gratitude to each one of you for being present," she said, her voice resonating with passion.

"We stand at a remarkable juncture, holding the potential not only to sustain our family's legacy but to launch it into a new era of innovation and influence."

The board members' eyes darted around the room, their expressions filled with intrigue as Rachel continued to paint a vivid picture of their proposed transformation.

"Inspired by insights gleaned from our family legacy, we have crafted a comprehensive strategy to position ourselves as trailblazers in sustainable technology and social entrepreneurship. This strategic shift will involve diversifying our investments and integrating innovative technologies into every facet of our operations."

Luke scrutinizes the board's reactions, noting a blend of skepticism and interest.

Mr. Thompson, a conservative member, leaned in, his hands clasped together. "Rachel, while your enthusiasm is commendable, such a substantial transition demands planning and considerable resources. How do you intend to mitigate the associated risks?"

Before responding, Rachel paused, her eyes searching for the right words. "I understand your concerns, Mr. Thompson. Our strategy incorporates thorough risk evaluations with a phased approach to implementation. We aim to kick-start new initiatives in select operational segments with growth potential, thus minimizing possible disruptions. We plan to collaborate with leading experts and innovators in the field to navigate this transition successfully."

A hush fell over the room as the board contemplated Rachel's words.

Luke stepped in, reinforcing the proposal. "This is not just about reshaping our business but about ensuring its continued relevance and prosperity in an evolving market. By embracing innovation, we can unlock fresh opportunities while upholding the cherished values of our family."

Mr. Thompson exhales, his demeanor softening. "Change is never simple, especially for a company entrenched in tradition. I discern the promise within your vision. I am keen to delve deeper into the specifics of your proposal."

Rachel and Luke dedicated an hour to their blueprint, outlining eco-friendly product lines, renewable energy investments, and a social impact fund supporting community-driven enterprises. Their plan also featured strategies to enhance employee involvement and growth, fostering a culture characterized by innovation and collaboration.

After the presentation, Rachel senses the room's atmosphere becoming more positive, with board members discussing the advantages and obstacles of the proposed transformation.

Finally, Mr. Thompson signals to conclude the meeting.

"I think there's a lot to discuss. Your proposal is bold and visionary. I appreciate your embodiment of our founding principles. Let's meet next week to discuss and decide."

As the board members exited, Rachel and Luke shared relieved smiles.

Sarah's heart raced as she stood outside the boardroom. The board members' expressions hinted at a victory for Rachel and Luke. The chatter among members as they exited confirmed her suspicions.

She got supercurious when she saw Luke looking at her.

"Did they agree to your proposal?" Her voice carries a mix of hope and excitement, eager to hear the outcome of their hard work and dedication.

Luke conveyed optimism and accomplishment in his words to her with a sense of pride and satisfaction, "We have made progress."

In that moment, a sense of achievement filled the air, setting the stage for even greater successes to come.

Sarah reaches for Luke's hand, her eyes shimmering with pride and her voice brimming with admiration.

"You both have done an exceptional job. Your impact is already substantial."

Rachel nods with a blend of relief and resolve in her gaze. "Thank you, Sarah. This is only the beginning. We have unlocked a realm of possibilities, and it falls to us to see them materialize."

Rachel and Luke fortify their initiatives by refining their proposal, gathering data, and contacting collaborators for guidance and cooperation.

Prepared for the board meeting with a united and determined mindset. They face the upcoming challenges, drawing strength from their shared vision and dedication, ready to lead their family business toward a new era of growth and influence.

Before the meeting began, Luke turned to Rachel, his gratitude transparent in his eyes. "Rachel, I am grateful that we are embarking on this journey together. Regardless of the outcome, I am proud of our achievements."

Rachel's eyes reflected his sentiment as she smiled back. "Thanks, Luke. With our family's support, we are an unstoppable force when united."

Upon entering the boardroom, the weight of a promising future lies before them.

Despite the hurdles they knew awaited them, they are resolute in their commitment to forge a path characterized by innovation, solidarity, and enduring impact.

Chapter 18

Building Bridges - Uniting the Community for a Stronger Tomorrow

Sarah and Luke stood amidst the tranquility of their family estate's garden, reminiscing about the path that led them to this moment. An ominous rumble beneath their feet shattered the peace they felt, exchanging startled looks as the ground trembled. The earth protested, the vibrations intensifying with each passing second.

"What was that?" Luke's voice tinged with concern as he tightened his hold on Sarah's hand. Before she could respond, another powerful tremor shook the ground, causing trees to sway and distant cries of alarm to reach their ears. Sarah realized they were amidst a natural disaster.

"We must make our way to the hospital," she said, her heart racing with a blend of fear and determination. Some people will need our help. "Let's go. We will do whatever it takes to ensure everyone's safety."

After gathering emergency supplies and informing their family members, they hurried to St. Anthony's. The scene that greeted them was chaotic, the emergency room filling up with injured individuals.

Sarah and Luke sprang into action, working in harmony with medical personnel and volunteers to prioritize patients and deliver vital care.

As Sarah navigated through the emergency room, offering aid and words of solace, she noticed Dr. Rivera overseeing a team of nurses. "How are we holding up, Dr. Rivera?" she asked.

Dr. Rivera, wiping sweat from her brow, said. "We're stretched, but managing, we are setting up an external triage area to cater to the overflow."

Sarah acknowledged this, her mind racing with the enormity of the impending task. "I will coordinate the external triage. Luke, can you support Dr. Rivera here?"

Without hesitation, Luke said, "I'm on it."

Sarah supervised the triage area amidst destruction and panic, witnessing acts of kindness and resilience within the community. With volunteers and medical personnel, she made the hospital's parking lot an efficient triage center.

Despite the grim circumstances, a sense of pride swelled within Sarah as she witnessed the united and resolute response of the community. They stood strong together, prepared to surmount this crisis.

As the number of injured individuals increased, Sarah's responsibilities grew. She administered first aid, offered comfort, and provided guidance, always keeping Luke and the safety of their loved ones in the forefront of her thoughts.

Even though Luke's thoughts occasionally turned to business, his goal was to protect lives and uphold the hospital's operations. Amidst a flurry of hospital activity, playing a crucial role in critical procedures and patient stabilization.

Hours later, Sarah and Luke reconvened in the hospital corridor, exhausted yet steadfast in purpose. "How are things?" Luke asked. "It's challenging, but we are coping. The community's unity is truly remarkable." Sarah said in a weary voice.

Luke's determination to assist those in need, he said. "We will not let this calamity defeat us. We will rebuild stronger than before."

A harried nurse interrupted their moment of solidarity, informing them of a developing situation at the riverfront. Without hesitation, Sarah and Luke committed to addressing the impending crisis, steeling themselves for the forthcoming challenge.

Upon reaching the riverfront, they encountered scenes of urgency and distress as floodwaters surged. Collaborating with local authorities and responders, they organized evacuation efforts, extending aid to the most vulnerable and using makeshift rafts to rescue stranded individuals.

As dawn approached and the waters receded, a fatigued yet resolute Sarah and Luke surveyed the aftermath. The town lay ravaged, yet its spirit remained unbroken.

"We did it," Luke said with a mix of relief and weariness. "But our path to recovery is just beginning."

Sarah, filled with pride for their community's resilience, affirmed, "Together, we will rebuild."

After going through a major ordeal together, Sarah and Luke developed a deep connection with their townspeople, who became their pillars of support.

Filled with a contemplative sense of their journey and the meaningful change they were enacting, they gazed out at the ruins, anticipating what the future held.

The hospital precinct was alive with activity, the bustling sounds of people working together to lend a helping hand. Engrossed in their own musings, the sound of footsteps startled them, drawing nearer, breaking their concentration.

A tall man emerged from the crowd, and Sarah recognized him right away. Mr. Thomas Grant is a respected local leader known for his contributions to community development and dedication to social causes.

As Sarah stepped forward to greet him, she extended her hand toward Mr. Grant, a welcoming gesture in her body language. "I feel incredibly honored to have the opportunity to see you here."

Mr. Grant smiled, his eyes twinkling with a mixture of wisdom and enthusiasm. "Please, call me Thomas. I've been following your work closely, and I must say, it's truly inspiring. We share a similar vision for the community, and I'd like to discuss how we can work together to bridge some gaps between your team and the community."

Luke and Sarah exchanged hopeful glances. "We'd love to hear your thoughts," Luke said, gesturing for Thomas to join them at one of the garden benches.

As they sat down, Thomas outlined his ideas. "I've seen firsthand how effective collaborations between local leaders and passionate individuals like yourselves can create lasting change. You have the resources and the vision, and I have the connections and understanding of the community's needs. Together, we can ensure that our efforts are not only impactful but also sustainable."

Sarah nodded, her excitement growing. "We need someone who can help us build stronger relationships with the community. Your experience and insights would be invaluable."

Thomas continued, "I've already spoken with several community leaders who are eager to support your foundation. It's important for them to see their voices being heard and concerns addressed. Trust is key, and we can build that trust by being transparent and actively engaging with community leaders who are eager to support your foundation. We need to show them we are listening to their voices and addressing their concerns."

Luke leaned forward, his interest piqued. "What do you suggest our next steps should be, Thomas?"

"First, we need to host a community forum," Thomas proposed. "Invite local leaders, residents, and anyone interested in contributing to the foundation's mission. This will provide a platform for open dialogue, where we can listen to their ideas and address any concerns they might have."

Sarah agreed. "That's a wonderful idea. We can also use this opportunity to showcase the progress we've made and the future projects we're planning."

Thomas nodded with a thoughtful expression on his face. "Exactly. We should establish a community advisory board comprising trusted members from various backgrounds. This board will ensure that the community has a direct role in decision-making processes, fostering a sense of ownership and involvement."

Luke smiled, feeling a renewed sense of purpose. "Thank you, Thomas. Your guidance is exactly what we need to strengthen our bond with the community. Let's plan the forum and reach out to potential advisory board members immediately."

With a simple plan in place, Sarah, Luke, and Thomas spent the next few days organizing the community forum. They reached out to local leaders, residents, and key stakeholders, emphasizing the importance of their participation. Many responded with an outpouring of positive feedback to the invitation, expressing their eagerness to attend and contribute.

Excitement and anticipation filled the forum venue that day. The spacious community center was the venue for the event, where the organizers adorned it with informational displays and photographs showcasing the foundation's work. Sarah and Luke mingled with the attendees, engaging in heartfelt conversations and listening to their stories.

Thomas took the stage to welcome everyone. "Thank you all for being here today. This forum marks the beginning of a deeper partnership between the foundation and our community. We're here to listen, to share, and to collaborate on projects that will uplift and empower us all."

The forum proceeded with various speakers, including local leaders, who voiced their support and offered constructive feedback. Sarah and Luke presented their vision for the foundation, highlighting the recent projects and outlining plans. The crowd responded with enthusiasm, and the sense of unity was palpable.

During the open discussion, a young woman stood up and introduced herself. "I'm Maria Rodriguez, and I've been working with underprivileged youth in our neighborhood. I see potential in what the foundation is doing, but I also see opportunities to engage our young people more actively in these initiatives."

Sarah radiated a smile and nodded. "Thank you, Maria. We would love to hear your ideas on how we can involve the youth and make a greater impact together."

Maria proposed creating mentorship programs and community service projects that could empower young people and their peers to take an active role in their development.

People supported her suggestions, and Maria would be an invaluable addition to the advisory board.

The forum concluded on a high note, with many attendees volunteering to take part in future projects and join the advisory board.

Thomas, Sarah, and Luke felt a deep sense of accomplishment and optimism as they witnessed the community's passion and commitment.

As the evening drew to a close, Thomas pulled Sarah and Luke aside. "You've done an incredible job today. The community is ready to stand with you, and together, we can achieve successful things. Remember, this is just the beginning. Building these relationships will take continuous effort, but the rewards will be immeasurable."

Sarah and Luke thanked Thomas for his support and guidance. With his help, they laid the groundwork for a future filled with hope, cooperation, and positive change. The bonds they had formed with the community would serve as the foundation for their ongoing efforts to create a legacy of unity and resilience.

Hand in hand, Sarah and Luke felt a deep connection with their mission as they left the venue. With the community's support and their strong partnership, they believed they could overcome any challenge. Together, they would continue to build a brighter future, one step at a time.

Chapter 19

Building Dreams and Embracing Surprises

After dedicating so much time to helping their community recover from the recent natural disaster, Sarah and Luke have become exhausted.

As they arrived home, the comforting sight of their cozy house greeted them, bathed in the warm glow of the setting sun.

Luke opens the door and turns to Sarah, saying, "We need time to recharge. I'll make dinner while you take it easy."

Sarah is grateful for his thoughtfulness and says, "I appreciate the offer, but I'm happy to help."

With a weary yet satisfied smile, they entered through the front door, feeling the weight of the day slip away. Their sanctuary welcomed them with the soothing sound of the air conditioning's soft hum and the steady ticking of the clock.

Sarah, feeling relaxed, fills her glass with a rich red wine in the kitchen and offers, "Would you care for a glass too?"

"Absolutely," Luke replies. "After today, I could use a little relaxation."

"I can't wait to sink into the cozy couch and enjoy a movie after dinner," Sarah says to Luke.

Before going to bed, they enjoyed a delicious dinner and watched an engaging movie.

Sarah wakes up early the next morning, giving Luke the chance to sleep in. The intensity of yesterday's activities has left her feeling less than her best.

Sarah begins her day by indulging in a steaming cup of brewed coffee, relishing its rich aroma and savoring the warmth that radiates from the mug. With the enveloping scent bringing her comfort, she steps outside onto the tranquil back deck, hoping to discover solace and gain a new perspective.

Sarah takes in the peaceful surroundings, feeling a sense of calm wash over her as she reflects on yesterday's events. She reminds herself that the challenges are integral to her career path, acknowledging that her chosen profession will fill many more days with demanding and lengthy hours, but she remains steadfast in her commitment.

Luke awoke feeling refreshed and full of energy. The extra sleep had done wonders for him. As he stepped outside, he found Sarah delighting in the serene stillness of the early morning. The soft caress of the gentle breeze brought a sense of tranquility. He couldn't resist joining her on the deck to bask in the peaceful start of the day.

"How did you rest last night?" he asks. She takes a sip of her coffee, sets it down, and says, "I slept soundly, but I'm considering staying home today to get some extra rest. I'm not feeling like myself."

He leans in, planting a soft kiss on her cheek. "Take a break and relax. I have some office tasks that require my attention, so I'll be away for a few hours."

As he makes his way to the office, Luke's phone buzzes with an incoming call from Thomas.

"Morning, Luke. I am interested in meeting with you to discuss the next phase of our project further."

Luke expresses his interest. "That sounds fantastic! When would you like to meet?"

"How about tomorrow? We can meet at the Corner Cafe and have lunch."

"Count on me to be there at noon," Luke assured.

As he made his way back from the office, he couldn't help but feel overwhelmed by the mounting responsibilities he and Sarah were facing. The new cardiac wing project, the global initiative, and the community program had all surged into a significant workload.

Luke felt surprised when he walked into the house and saw Sarah lying on the sofa, looking unwell.

He expresses his concern for her well-being and asks, "How are you feeling?"

Sarah shares with him, "I'm feeling a little queasy and tired."

"Is there anything I can do to help you feel more comfortable? A soothing cup of warm peppermint tea might be nice for you right now."

In the kitchen, he prepares a comforting cup of peppermint tea for her to ease her discomfort.

Despite feeling unwell the next morning, Sarah faced a challenging day at the hospital.

Sarah's weary footsteps reverberate through the sterile corridor as she moves forward. Upon reaching the nurses' station, she locks eyes with Dr. Rivera. Despite Sarah's efforts to mask her fatigue, her expression doesn't escape Dr. Rivera's astute observation.

Dr. Rivera recommends that she have a check-up to determine whether her blood levels are low. Sarah heeds Dr. Rivera's advice and goes to the lab to get her blood tested.

Meanwhile, Luke meets with Thomas during lunch to discuss the next steps that are necessary to bring the community together.

Days later, Sarah received the results of her blood labs, scanning through the report with bated breath. Relief washes over her as she reads. Everything appears normal. However, her heart skips when her eyes land on one glaring detail—she is pregnant. Shock and disbelief course through her as she comes to grips with the unexpected news, her mind racing with emotions and questions about the journey ahead.

As Sarah's heart races with anticipation, she dials Luke's number to share the life-changing news. When he answers, a mixture of nerves and excitement fills Sarah's voice. "Luke, I'm pregnant! We are going to have a baby!" Luke's joy was palpable through the phone. "That thrills me, Sarah. We are going to be wonderful parents together." His unwavering support and confidence in their future filled her with comfort and security, knowing they were in this together.

Sarah and Luke's upcoming addition to the family fills them with immense joy. Even with all the excitement, they never lose sight of their goal to make a difference in their community. Sarah and Luke reveal just how selfless and caring they are by dedicating themselves to the healthcare project at St. Anthony's and their determination to build a new cardiac wing. Their devotion extends to their family and others' well-being.

Three months later, Luke and Sarah enjoy a peaceful afternoon on their deck. The persistent ringing of Luke's phone interrupted the serenity. With a sense of urgency, he picks up to hear Chad's eager but concerned voice on the other end.

Chad, the representative from the engineering company overseeing the construction of the new cardiac wing, updates Luke and seeks his input, pulling him back into the world of blueprints and steel beams.

The call jolts Luke out of his tranquil moment, reminding him of the significant project at hand, blending the peaceful present with the weighty responsibility for the future.

Luke hangs up and turns to Sarah. "I can't control my excitement! We are looking around five moths to the completion of the cardiac unit."

"Luke, that's amazing! When we complete the cardiac wing, it will revolutionize the experience for our patients. With the additional space and resources, our cardiac patients are going to receive even better care. I can't wait to see the positive impact it will have!"

"It's going to take the quality of care we offer to a whole new level and have a significant impact on their recovery," Luke said.

Sarah agrees, "Absolutely. I'm so proud to see all the hard work paying off. Thank you for supporting my dreams and overseeing the process."

Luke admires her enthusiasm. "Of course, Sarah. We have made a successful team, and I couldn't have done it without your support. I'm looking forward to seeing the cardiac unit finished and the positive impact it will have on patients."

Sarah's phone pings with a flurry of notifications out of nowhere. She glances at the screen and is stunned to see a reminder about her long-awaited appointment with her experienced and friendly gynecologist, Dr. Shelley Long, tomorrow! Amidst her hectic schedule at the hospital, she had forgotten about this important appointment.

"Are you planning to accompany me to the appointment?" Sarah asked. With a warm smile, Luke replies, "I wouldn't miss it for the world."

The next morning, Sarah and Luke get ready to head out for Sarah's appointment. Sarah can barely contain her excitement as she tells Luke, "Today, we get to see our baby for the first time during the ultrasound with Dr. Long!"

As they make their way to Dr. Long's office, they find themselves entranced by the magnificent sights that surround them. Towering mountains stand proud in the distance, lush green valleys stretch out, scattered with vibrant wildflowers swaying in the gentle breeze. The meandering river flows along the landscape, providing a peaceful and awe-inspiring moment before their appointment. A profound sense of serenity and gratitude for the natural world fills them. Thankful for the chance to behold such breathtaking beauty.

As they entered Dr. Long's office, they noticed that many expectant mothers and fathers occupied the chairs in the waiting room. The room exuded a cheerful and welcoming atmosphere.

The nurse opens the door and calls her name to be seen. She and Luke follow her to the exam room.

"Hi, I'm Pam, Dr. Long's PA. Have a seat, and Dr. Long will be with you in just a few minutes."

Sarah and Luke make themselves comfortable in the spacious padded chairs.

Dr. Long taps on the door before stepping inside. "Hello, I'm Dr. Long. How are you feeling today?" she inquires, glancing at Sarah's chart.

Sarah's laughter fills the room as a wide grin spreads across her face. "I'm feeling fantastic, although I'm noticing that my clothes aren't fitting as perfectly as they used to," she says.

Dr. Long asks her to take a seat on the exam table. As she applies a cold gel to her stomach and reaches for a wand, she says, "Let's look at how your little one is growing."

She glides the monitor across her stomach. The rhythmic beeping fills the room, creating a mesmerizing soundtrack to the miracle of hearing the unborn child's heartbeat.

"Everything looks fantastic! I'll see you in a few months," Dr. Long says with a smile as she exits the room.

As Sarah and Luke leave Dr. Long's office, joy and hope fill them after hearing their baby's heartbeat. "There's a miracle growing inside you, Sarah," Luke says as he opens the car door for her.

Their journey is just starting as they embark on the incredible adventure of becoming parents, and soon, the new cardiac wing will become a remarkable reality.

Chapter 20

A Day of Dedication and Joy

Luke and Sarah accept an exclusive invitation to an interview about the latest technology and new features to raise the community's cardiac care level at St. Andrew's.

As the first light of dawn illuminates the horizon, Luke stirs from his sleep with the sound of chirping birds, breaking the peaceful silence.

He focuses on his interview with the local news network, getting ready to provide a detailed rundown of all the fantastic services that the facility will provide.

Sarah is up early and ready to leave for work when she hears Luke stirring in the adjacent room. She asks him, "Luke, what time is your interview today?"

Still in his robe, he walks into the kitchen. "Around 10 o'clock. Are you still joining me for the interview?"

"Of course, she says with a giggle, glancing at his tousled hair. I will make my rounds and catch up with you once I finish."

Luke takes a refreshing shower before making his way to the hospital. As he drives, he admires the surrounding scenery, immersing himself in the beauty of his community.

Luke pulled into the parking lot. The impressive design of the new cardiac wing amazes him. The sleek, modern structure stood tall, integrating with the hospital's architecture. Its large windows and curved lines gave it a sense of openness and fluidity, creating a feeling of hope and comfort for those entering the hospital.

He recalls the extensive effort he and Sarah have put into making Sarah's vision a reality.

"It is time to raise awareness in the community about the significance of setting up an innovative cardiac unit that has the potential to save lives. This interview aims to ensure that the community stays well-informed." He thought.

Sarah shows up a few minutes later. Luke embraces her and informs her that John is waiting for them in the lobby.

As Sarah and Luke start walking into the building, their interview host welcomes them. "Hi there, I am John. Are you all set to share the details of the exciting project you have been working on?" he asks.

With a gleam in his eye, Luke replies, "Absolutely! Let us dive right in."

"Luke and Sarah, thank you for joining us today," John says.

"Luke, can you give us some details about the new cardiac wing?"

"Yes, John, the new cardiac wing will have ultramodern equipment and technology, including advanced monitoring systems and specialized treatment rooms. We are also adding more patient rooms, dedicated cardiac rehabilitation facilities, and a more prominent family waiting area."

John listens, focusing on the project's aspects. "That is amazing. Having all these resources in one place will streamline patient care and improve outcomes. I am glad there will be an expansion for cardiac rehabilitation services."

Luke nods. "Yes, providing comprehensive care for our cardiac patients, from diagnosis to recovery, is essential. The new wing will also have a team of specialized cardiac nurses and doctors to ensure our patients receive the best possible care."

John replies, "That is fantastic. I am impressed with all the features and resources in the new wing. I cannot wait to see it all come together. Thank you for all your hard work in making this happen."

Sarah says, "It has been a team effort, John. I am grateful to have such dedicated colleagues by our side. I know the new cardiac wing will make a massive difference for our patients, and I am eager to see its positive impact on their health and well-being."

"Luke, will the new cardiac wing use the latest technologies to enhance patient care and outcomes?"

"We will have advanced monitoring systems to track vital signs in real-time and alert medical staff to any changes or abnormalities. These monitoring systems will allow them to provide immediate intervention and treatment when needed."

"That is impressive. Such advanced monitoring systems will improve patient safety and allow medical staff to respond quickly to emergencies. What are the added technologies included in the wing?" John asks.

Luke replies, "We will also have specialized imaging equipment, such as advanced cardiac MRI and CT scanners, to provide detailed images of the heart and blood vessels. Which will help doctors accurately diagnose and treat various cardiac conditions."

"When will the new cardiac unit open?" John asks.

"We are looking at a projected timeline of six weeks. The new equipment installation has started." Luke said.

John says with excitement in his voice. "I will be here with cameras rolling for the ribbon-cutting ceremony! Thank you for sharing the details of this project, Luke. The innovative technology will help our community."

"John, the collaborative effort put into this project has been remarkable. I am thankful to work alongside such dedicated colleagues. I am confident that the new cardiac wing will significantly affect our community," Luke said.

As Sarah and Luke left the interview, a whirl of thoughts engulfed them. They grapple with the lingering echoes of questions and their articulated responses. Doubts gnaw at them, questioning whether they had championed the merits of the new cardiac wing with the utmost eloquence. Had they conveyed how this innovative facility would revolutionize patient care? Would their passion and dedication shine through as brilliantly as they had envisioned?

Only time will reveal whether this pivotal interview will pave the path toward their aspirations or mark a mere diversion in their professional journeys.

Sarah's phone rings, and to her delight, it is Eleanor on the line. "Hey Eleanor, how are you feeling?" Sarah inquires with genuine concern.

Eleanor's warm voice responds, "I'm well, and you?"

Sarah cannot help but chuckle at Eleanor's inquiry, replying with a hint of humor, "Just getting bigger as we speak!"

Eleanor laughs, "Would love to catch up. Would you and Luke join me for dinner?" She asks.

"We would love to have dinner with you and catch up," Sarah replies.

"Perfect! Her voice filled the air with excitement. Will 7:00 work for you and Luke?" She asked.

"Yes, can we bring anything?" Sarah asked.

"Just your lovely selves. I will see you tonight." She replies.

Eleanor's warm invitation to catch up over dinner with her and Luke exudes a genuine connection. Her desire to spend quality time together and share a meal shows her appreciation for their company and the bond they all share.

This opportunity to enjoy each other's company over a delicious meal promises a delightful evening filled with laughter, conversation, and cherished memories.

On her way back to the hospital, Sarah's mind races with concern for her patients.

As she moves through the familiar corridors, she exchanges quick updates with the nursing staff, nodding to familiar faces.

Meanwhile, Luke sat across from Rachael in the office, a sense of anticipation in the air as they discussed the new vendors crucial to the expansion project.

Their conversation ebbs and flows, ideas bouncing off one another, charting a course toward success.

Despite the different settings, Sarah and Luke, driven by the same dedication to their work, are determined to affect those they serve.

As the late afternoon sun dips below the horizon, Sarah and Luke meet at home before heading to Eleanor's for dinner. Despite their fatigue, the day's excitement lingers, prompting discussions about preparing the nursery for their upcoming arrival.

"We should start getting the nursery ready," Sarah tells Luke.

"We'll tackle it over the weekend," he responds.

Sarah sighs, "Time is slipping away. Our workload and the new cardiac wing have been overwhelming."

"Let's have a delightful evening with Eleanor to unwind and rejuvenate," he suggested while grabbing his car keys.

In agreement, she says, "That is a plan. We should go."

Heading towards Eleanor's residence, they travel alongside the picturesque river, enjoying the serene views.

Eleanor's charming bungalow sits nestled in a quaint riverside plot of land.

The winding driveway leads to her vibrant home, with bold red shutters and colorful flowers all around, creating an enchanting sight.

Eleanor senses their approach and steps onto the front porch, eager to greet them and looking forward to spending quality time together.

Sarah lends a hand tidying up the table after dinner while Luke relaxes on the front porch, savoring the evening.

Sarah and Eleanor step out onto the porch, where Luke updates Eleanor on the latest developments in the cardiac unit. Eleanor beams with pride at their achievements and looks forward to becoming a great-aunt.

Sarah and Luke could not wait for the weekend to arrive. They could not wait to paint the nursery and get everything ready for their little one! The beautiful sunshine and the soft breeze outside only added to their joyful anticipation.

Luke is standing outside the nursery door when his phone rings. It is Chad, the engineer overseeing the cardiac wing project.

"Hey Chad, how are you?" He asks. "I am doing fantastic! I would like to share some exciting news. We are looking to finish it in four weeks! The project is moving faster than we thought," he said.

"Wow! That is news to hear," Luke replies.

"I will call you in a few weeks to give you another update. If you have questions, call me," Chad says.

Luke cannot help but burst into laughter as he catches sight of Sarah covered in a spectacular explosion of colorful paint from head to toe! His laugh is hearty, saying to her, "I hope that comes off before you head back to work." Sarah chuckles in response and asks, "What did Chad need?"

As she wiped the paint from her nose with a cloth, Luke revealed, "Chad just told me they are early for completion! Looks like the construction may wrap up in four weeks or even sooner."

"Luke, it is getting real!" she exclaimed, her excitement clear in her voice.

Amid their hectic schedules, Sarah and Luke consistently carve out time to sit together and organize their upcoming commitments. A gentle breeze heralds the changing seasons as they efficiently manage their busy calendars.

While arranging the guest list for St. Andrew's Hospital's New Cardiac Wing grand opening, Sarah and Luke take a moment to appreciate and recognize the key figures instrumental in bringing the project to life.

"Let's ensure Thomas speaks at the ceremony to emphasize the positive impact this will have on countless lives," Sarah asserts.

Luke nods in agreement, signaling his approval. "Thomas has been pivotal in coordinating the event and attracting essential contributors," he affirms.

Sarah explores additional invites with Dr. Blake in mind. "I'll reach out to Dr. Blake for a speech; as the Cardiology Head, his presence is essential alongside his team," she mentions.

Luke confirms, "I'll contact Thomas while you contact Dr. Blake."

Anticipation fills the air as Luke skillfully prepares rich hot cocoa, enveloping them in the comforting scent of chocolate. Engrossed in meticulously drafting the list of esteemed speakers, Sarah's dedication shines through in her focused expression and steady pen taps.

Sarah and Luke extended invitations to Dr. Blake and Thomas the following week.

Dr. Blake and Thomas are delighted to take part in the Grand Opening, infusing the community with hope and promise by unveiling the new cardiac wing.

Luke is preparing for the grand opening when his phone suddenly rings. Hesitating for a moment at the unknown number, he finally decides to pick it up. "Hello, this is Luke speaking," he answers.

"Hello, Luke. I am Todd Hamby from Environmental Health and Safety. I want to arrange a visit to inspect the cardiac facility. Could we find a convenient time for you to meet?"

Luke glances at his calendar to check his schedule. "I'm free on Tuesday, anytime after lunch," he mentions.

"Can we arrange to meet around two o'clock?" he inquires.

"Certainly, that time suits me," Luke confirms.

Sarah is currently in her third trimester of pregnancy, and as her baby continues to grow and develop, she has begun to feel the physical effects. Due to the added weight and size of her baby bump, finding a comfortable sleeping position has become increasingly challenging, making it more difficult for her to move around the hospital, especially while attending to her patients.

As Luke and Todd embark on their environmental inspection, they meticulously ensure that every aspect of the facility adheres to the highest standards. Luke finds himself thoroughly impressed as he explores the facility, appreciating the meticulous construction work clearly throughout. As he enters the expansive atrium, he is captivated by the soaring ceiling and the soft glow from the skylights, enveloping the space in a welcoming and tranquil ambiance. Next to the atrium, a charming coffee shop awaits, offering a delightful selection of pastries and light sandwiches. Plush, cushioned sofas provide a cozy and inviting space for families to come together and relax. Continuing down the corridor, they come across a tranquil chapel, offering a serene sanctuary where families can seek solace and offer their prayers.

The new building will officially open next week, following the successful completion of a comprehensive inspection process to ensure that it meets all necessary standards for safety and functionality. Sarah and Luke are working diligently to finalize the guest speakers and ensure everything is in place for the grand opening and ribbon-cutting ceremony on the anticipated day.

Sarah's long-cherished vision of setting up an innovative cardiac wing at the hospital finally materializes into reality.

Today is a momentous occasion as they celebrate the highly expected grand opening of the New Cardiac Wing. This significant event begins an exciting journey filled with opportunities to connect with our community and provide exceptional service to our cardiac patients. Sarah and Luke awaken feeling rejuvenated and overjoyed as they see their dream materialize. The day promises to be truly spectacular.

Sarah and Luke are on the stage alongside respected physicians and local officials, ready to unveil the new facility to the community.

As Luke walks confidently towards the microphone, the room falls into a hushed silence in anticipation of his words. He addresses the gathered audience with a steady gaze, his voice poised and resolute, ready to captivate their attention.

"Thank you for being here, he says.

"Today, we gather as a community to celebrate a shared vision that has come to fruition through your generous contributions of time, support, and finances. I thank my wife, Sarah, for bravely pursuing her longstanding dream."

[applause]

"It is an honor to introduce our first guest speaker, Mr. Thomas Grant, a highly esteemed leader within our community."

[applause]

Taking the stage, Thomas addresses the audience, starting with a polite acknowledgment, "Thank you, Luke."

In response, Luke nods appreciatively and replies, "Thank you for joining us, Thomas."

Thomas commends Sarah and Luke for their unwavering commitment to this vital project.

He emphasizes the importance of specific patient confidentiality protocols to enhance standards.

"The safeguarding of patient information, utilization of cutting-edge imaging technology, and secure medical data encryption," he emphasizes. "I will defer to Dr. Blake for further insights on these protocols."

As Dr. Blake approaches the microphone, his words flow with eloquence as he delves into a comprehensive explanation of each protocol, captivating the audience with his depth of knowledge.

"Access to advanced imaging technology will allow more precise and personalized patient treatment plans, significantly affecting their care and outcomes. The combination of advanced monitoring systems and imaging technology will help us deliver the highest quality of care to cardiac patients, improving the level of care we can provide in the cardiac wing."

[The audience is captivated and hangs on every spoken word.]

"Patient data security is our top priority in the new cardiac wing. We have strict protocols to keep all patient information confidential and secure, including encrypted electronic records, secure access controls, regular security audits, and staff training. Patient data is only shared on a need-to-know basis among authorized healthcare providers within the wing, using secure communication channels and strict guidelines."

[The audience applauds as he gracefully hands the spotlight back to Luke.]

"Luke expresses his gratitude to Dr. Blake as the ushers unveil the vibrant red ribbon extending across the stage."

The hospital administrator passes a large pair of scissors to Luke and Sarah, who cut the ribbon together. Luke announces, "The brand-new, innovative cardiac wing is now open! We are excited to welcome patients and families needing exceptional cardiac care."

The room erupts with enthusiastic cheers and applause from all present.

Sarah and Luke return home feeling proud and exhausted after a long, exhilarating day at the grand opening event. Sarah is bubbling with pride after a fantastic day, and she cannot wait to dive into her thrilling new role at the forefront cardiac unit.

Sarah reclines on the sofa, feeling the baby's lively kicks and somersaults. She gently places Luke's hand on her belly and remarks, "Seems like someone is excited about the cardiac wing, too," her eyes gleaming.

Luke senses joy as he feels the baby's movements within Sarah. The wonder of new life developing inside her is genuinely exceptional!

"I have a feeling we might have a little acrobat in the making," he says with a wide grin.

Sarah giggles while the baby playfully stretches across her belly, its tiny feet reaching as far as they can.

"I cannot wait for our little one to arrive! If it is a girl, I would love to honor my mother and grandmother by naming her Arabella Florence."

Luke gazes at her with a hint of sentiment in his eyes. "I like that name. What if it's a boy?" he asked.

Sarah paused, reflecting for a moment. "I think Lucas Benjamin is a name that pays tribute to you and my father."

"That name resonates well with me," he remarked.

Sarah signals to Luke that she is ready for bed, feeling a yawn escape. She has an appointment scheduled with Dr. Long in the morning. She predicts the next few weeks will pass quickly, and they will finally meet their little one.

Sarah gets up early, dresses, and heads for her appointment with Dr. Long.

The waiting room is full of expectant mothers when she arrives.

As Sarah patiently waits in the cozy waiting room, the nurse gently calls out her name and leads her to the comforting atmosphere of the exam room. Dr. Long walks in with a warm smile, exchanging pleasantries with Sarah before diving into the medical consultation. After inquiring about Sarah's overall well-being, the kind-hearted doctor attentively listens as Sarah expresses her eager anticipation to meet her little one.

Dr. Long performs a thorough examination and delicately explains that Sarah's cervix has started to thin. This positive sign shows that the much-anticipated birth may only be a few weeks away. With the utmost care and concern, Dr. Long recommends that Sarah prioritize rest and avoid overexertion to ensure a smooth and healthy progression toward childbirth.

Before Sarah leaves, Dr. Long schedules another appointment for the following week to closely check her well-being and the progression of her pregnancy.

After getting into her car, Sarah calls Luke to update him on her appointment with Dr. Long.

Surprisingly, the call went straight to voicemail, prompting her to leave him a message.

"Just a quick update: my appointment went smoothly. Let us catch up for lunch so I can fill you in. Feel free to give me a call when you have a chance to check this message."

She drives to the cardiac unit to complete some paperwork before taking time off for the birth of her baby. She hopes to continue working, if possible, right up to the due date.

"Dr. Blake visits her, lightly tapping on the door before entering the room. "I've brought over these patient files for you. Knowing that your birth-related leave is approaching, I will manage the upcoming surgical cases," he says."

Exhaling with relief, she expresses, "I have complete faith in your ability to care for these patients. Your competence impresses me. Thank you for reviewing the files."

"You are welcome, Sarah," he replied.

As she was organizing the files in the cabinet, she was surprised when he asked if she could help with a transplant the following week.

Determinedly, she responds, "I would be happy to assist as long as it does not interfere with my appointment with Dr. Long on Tuesday."

"The surgery is planned for Thursday morning." He replies.

"I will be there to assist you," she confirms with a smile.

When Sarah left her office, Dr. Blake sparked her excitement about participating in a groundbreaking heart transplant under his mentorship.

Sarah's thoughts swirl as she envisions a future in cardiothoracic surgery. Her thoughts are interrupted when her phone pings with a text from Luke.

"Meet me at the cardiac unit's new coffee shop."

She replies, "I will meet you there. On my way!"

Luke warmly embraces Sarah, kissing her cheek tenderly when she arrives in the lobby,

He asks about her appointment with Dr. Long and then smoothly transitions into asking about her day.

Sarah finds a table while Luke places their order.

When he returns with their meals, he carefully places the tray on the table and sits beside her. Eager to share, she vividly recounts her recent appointment with Dr. Long.

"Dr. Long says that my cervix is beginning to efface. I have another appointment to see her again next week to monitor my progress."

Full of questions and anxiety, he asks, "What does this mean? Is everything okay with the baby?"

She reaches across the table, offering a reassuring pat on his arm as she explains, "After the baby engages in the pelvis, it gradually drops closer to the cervix, which then softens, shortens, and becomes thinner in preparation for delivery."

Fascinated by her words, he asks as if he is hearing this for the first time. "How is it measured?"

As she drinks her water, she pauses and says, "Percentages measure the cervix effacement."

Luke's expression turns puzzled. "Percentages?" he asks.

"Yes, here is an example: When the cervix is thinning, 50% means halfway, and at 100% effacement, the cervix is paper-thin, and labor is usually close."

The reality of impending fatherhood fills him with excitement, nervousness, and a sense of responsibility as he acknowledges the significant life change that is about to happen.

Sarah comforts him, assuring him that everything is under control and that the baby will come when ready.

"Dr. Blake came to see me earlier. He asked if I would assist him on a heart transplant next week."

Luke looks at her with concern and asks, "Will standing for that long be in your best interest, given that the baby could soon be born?"

"I understand your concerns. I will be fine; I can take a break and sit down as needed," Sarah says.

Luke smiles, " I will support your decision if you think you will be okay."

"She responds, "I appreciate your support, thank you!"

Sarah is thrilled to have the chance to help Dr. Blake with a heart transplant procedure. Being in the operating room with such a respected surgeon inspires her to develop her skills and knowledge further.

When Sarah returns to her office, she dives into her medical journals to prepare to support Dr. Blake in any way he needs.

Meanwhile, Luke is completing matters with Rachel at the office. The recent merger has succeeded, and a few documents await his signature to seal the deal.

"I am happy to hear about the completion of the new cardiac unit. Rachel says to Luke.

Luke settles back in his desk chair, firmly lacing his fingers, and remarks, "Yes, I am as well. I have several tasks to take care of before the arrival of the little one."

Rachel is eagerly looking forward to becoming an aunt soon. "How is Sarah doing? I haven't had a chance to catch up with her lately," she inquires.

Luke's face lights up with a smile, his eyes sparkling excitedly. "She is as prepared as she can be; she's fully committed to patient care," he says.

"That is great to hear; keeping busy during the final weeks of pregnancy can help time pass more quickly. However, it is important for Sarah to prioritize rest as well," Rachel responds with concern.

"I will make sure she takes the time to rest," he responds.

As the evening falls, Sarah and Luke double-check the nursery to ensure everything is ready to welcome their new arrival. Sarah prepares her suitcase while Luke positions the baby carrier by the front door in anticipation of the big day.

"It looks like we are ready to meet our little one," Luke tells Sarah, reminding her to take several breaks throughout the day and not overexert herself.

"I will," she says. I have my appointment tomorrow with Dr. Long. Will you be able to go with me? She asks.

Luke stands behind Sarah, wrapping his arms around her midsection, feeling the gentle movements of the baby inside. With a reassuring tone, he promises, "I'll adjust my schedule to be there for you."

Sarah leans her head back against his shoulder, sighing with relief. "Thank you," she says, placing her hands around his.

Dr. Long examined Sarah the following day and shared that she was approximately 50% effaced. Reassuringly, she mentioned that Sarah's progress is typical and predicted the baby's arrival by the same time next week.

Sarah and Luke listened closely as Dr. Long continued instructing Sarah.

"Rest up. I will see you at the office on Tuesday unless we happen to meet earlier at the hospital." She says with a comforting, gentle smile.

After leaving Dr. Long's office, Sarah informs Luke that she plans to assist Dr. Blake on Thursday. Luke emphasizes the importance of taking breaks if she goes ahead with it. A heart transplant procedure with no complications usually lasts about four hours. Sarah assures Luke that she will remember to take necessary breaks.

Sarah eagerly wakes up early, excited to get to the hospital. Bursting with energy, she steps out of her car and strides through the refreshing morning breeze, ready for the day ahead.

She enters the hospital and goes straight to the third floor for the operating room. After taking a quick elevator ride, she goes to the locker room to put on surgical scrubs.

The nurses and staff are preparing the operating room for Dr. Blake's surgery.

Sarah enters the operating room and heads to the sink to scrub her hands meticulously. The patient awaits the presence of the anesthesiologist and Dr. Blake to start the procedure. After washing his hands, Dr. Blake moves toward the operating table and affirms his readiness to begin. The patient slips into slumber as the anesthesia medicine drips through the IV.

Sarah watches Dr. Blake's hands expertly and precisely navigate the task, his unwavering focus driving his movements.

The quiet room is filled with the rhythmic beeping of monitors, creating a tense and anxious atmosphere. As the transplant nears completion, Sarah experiences a dull ache in her back from standing for hours. She decides to rest in the observation room before returning to assist Dr. Blake with closing the chest cavity during the final hour of surgery.

After surgically implanting the new heart, Dr. Blake skillfully reconnects it, enlisting Sarah's help to position the defibrillator paddles around the patient's revitalized heart. With precision, he charges the voltage to revive its beating rhythm.

Sarah is captivated as she sees the heart beginning to beat, and the steady rhythm on the monitor signals a successful implantation.

Dr. Blake announces, "We have a heartbeat," bringing about cheers from the nurses and staff in the room.

Sarah is excited as she helps Dr. Blake in closing the patient's chest cavity. As she leaves the operating room, she is aware of a persistent, dull ache in her back and legs.

After changing her clothes, she heads toward her office, where she reclines on the sofa, relieving the strain on her legs. Feeling a surge of pain, she calls Luke.

When Luke answers the phone, he can detect the distress in her voice. "Can you come pick me up? She asks, expressing uncertainty about driving home.

"Yes, I am on my way. Do I need to call Dr. Long? He asks.

"Not yet; wait until you get here, and let's see if I am feeling any better," she replied

Upon Luke's arrival, he assesses the situation and discerns that she is in labor. He promptly contacts Dr. Long, who recommends that he have her examined by one of the hospital's nurses.

He helps her in standing up, yet her legs are unsteady. He finds a wheelchair and escorts her to the obstetrics and gynecology department. Once there, a nurse settles her into an examination room and confirms that she is indeed experiencing labor.

The nurse pages Dr. Long and informs her of Sarah's labor.

Sarah's room bustled with nurses and aides moving back and forth, attaching monitors to her stomach and getting ready for the delivery.

Sarah gazes at the monitor, seeing each contraction's increasing intensity and frequency. She stays focused, regulating her breathing throughout. After three hours, the pain persists, growing stronger. Luke stands beside her, offering comfort and support.

After rechecking her dilation, the nurse confirmed Sarah was 8cm. "You're making great progress; it won't be much longer now," she reassured.

One more hour passes, and Sarah senses the need to push. The nurse says, "Hold on. Dr. Long is on her way. Don't push just yet."

When Dr. Long enters the room, her charming personality shines through. She asks Sarah, "Are we ready to meet this little one?"

Not feeling amused, Sarah replies, "Any time now!"

"Sarah, with the next contraction, let's push together now," encourages the doctor. Sarah responds with a strong push, her voice mingling with a cry of effort. "You're doing great, Sarah. Just one more powerful push," the doctor urges. Taking a deep breath, Sarah pushes with determination, releasing her breath as she does.

Overwhelmed with emotion, she senses a sudden rush as the room echoes with the cry of her newborn son. "It's a boy!" announces Dr. Long. The nurses swiftly attend to the baby while Dr. Long shifts her focus back to Sarah.

"You were incredible, Sarah. My heart is full," Luke whispers with tenderness, gently kissing her forehead.

The nurse gently hands the newborn to Sarah and Luke. As Sarah cradles him, tears of joy stream down her cheeks. With a tender voice, she whispers, "Hello, Lucas Benjamin! I am your mommy, and this is your daddy. We're overjoyed to meet you finally."

Sarah and Luke have achieved remarkable success in their careers, but their most significant accomplishment was embracing the role of parents.

Together, they have navigated a journey filled with highs and lows, their enduring friendship leading them to this significant moment. The opportunity to forge their legacy alongside their son, Lucas Benjamin, fills them with hope. Their legacy lives on through the dreams and aspirations of those who follow them.

www.ingramcontent.com/pod-product-compliance
Lightning Source LLC
Chambersburg PA
CBHW060930140726
47996CB00001B/454